OLD DESIRES

Joshua Kent infuriated Holly — he was arrogant, overbearing and convinced she was a good-for-nothing gold-digger! But even worse was his bombshell that her past was a complete fabrication. A new identity — and the inheritance which went with it — meant that Holly could embark on a fresh life for herself. But where did Joshua fit into the scheme of things? Was he just using the desire which flared between them to manipulate her? Only time would tell . . .

LIZ FIELDING

OLD DESIRES

Complete and Unabridged

LINFORD
Leicester

First published in Great Britain in 1994

First Linford Edition
published 2011

British Library CIP Data

Fielding, Liz.
   Old desires. - - (Linford romance library)
   1. Love stories.
   2. Large type books.
   I. Title II. Series
   823.9'14–dc22

ISBN 978–1–4448–0687–8

Published by
F. A. Thorpe (Publishing)
Anstey, Leicestershire

Set by Words & Graphics Ltd.
Anstey, Leicestershire
Printed and bound in Great Britain by
T. J. International Ltd., Padstow, Cornwall

This book is printed on acid-free paper

1

'Miss Carpenter?'

The enquiry was simply a formality. Holly had no doubt that the man on her doorstep, filling the entrance with his powerful presence, knew exactly who she was. In that, he had her at a disadvantage and she didn't much care for it, or for the quite unmistakable chill in his manner.

She had the quite definite feeling that, whatever the reason for his call, he would prefer not to be making it at all and she already wished she had kept to her usual habit of ignoring the doorbell when she was working. Except that this afternoon nothing was going right and she had almost welcomed the interruption.

Besides, one look had told her that this man would not have simply given up and gone away. Determination was written in every austere, finely chiselled line of his face, an intensity of purpose that hardened the sensual curve of his full lower lip.

'I'm Holly Carpenter,' she affirmed with an unconscious lift of her chin, wondering what this arrogant and very expensively groomed man could possibly want with her. A well-cut navy pin-striped suit gracing the square shoulders and lean, hard figure and the telling pale blue stripe of his tie betrayed that he was a long way from his City office. And his method of transport, if the gleaming silver Rolls at the kerb could be described in so plebeian a manner, was already attracting curtain-twitching attention from a window opposite.

Under the disapproving gaze of a pair of wintry grey eyes her paint-splattered smock, a rather grand word for a gaudy shirt bought at a jumble sale to cover her clothes while she worked, felt faintly ridiculous. But she firmly resisted the urge to snatch it off and bundle it into the nearest corner. She resisted too the almost overwhelming desire to rub her hands down the back of her jeans to wipe away any lingering trace of paint, blissfully unaware of the streak of umber that swooped across her wide forehead. But he did not offer his hand.

'Joshua Kent.' He introduced himself briefly and extended a card between two fingers.

Holly took the slip of white pasteboard. It bore his name and a London address that added to the aura of wealth that surrounded the man, but told her nothing useful. And a public-school tie and haughty manner were insufficient reason for her to let a total stranger into her home when she was on her own.

'I'm sorry, Mr Kent, I don't believe I know — '

'There is no reason why you should know me, Miss Carpenter. I would have telephoned prior to calling, but you aren't apparently listed.' His face showed very clearly what he thought of someone inconsiderate enough to have an unlisted number. Someone, that was, who lived in a very ordinary semi-detached house, in a very ordinary street.

Holly found considerable satisfaction in being able to answer, 'I'm not listed, Mr Kent, because I don't have a telephone.' She added, with grave humour, 'But I do have a letterbox. Perhaps you should avail yourself of that facility.' Her snub made not the slightest impression and the restrained anger in his voice was far more effective than any crude foot-in-door at halting her move to shut him out.

'My business is too urgent for a letter. I am here on behalf of Mary Graham.' His mouth tightened dangerously. 'The late Mary Graham.'

'Mary Graham?' Holly's forehead creased in the faintest frown. She could only recollect having met her mother's cousin once, but the occasion had left a vivid imprint on her young mind. It had been her seventh birthday. She had been having a party and everything was

4

wonderful. Then Mary Graham had arrived with a present, an expensive doll that she had wanted so much, begged for, but her mother had said they could not afford. She had impulsively thrown her arms around the woman's neck and hugged her. 'She's dead?' she asked.

'She died the night before last.' He was watchful, clearly expecting some response to this news. Certainly she felt a natural sadness at hearing of the death of anyone, but her mother was dead too and Mary Graham hadn't shown any interest then.

She regarded him steadily with golden, almond-slanting eyes. She could usually read a face but his expression was guarded, as if her reaction was too important to be influenced by his own expectations, and that bothered her.

For a long moment he returned her look, holding it with eyes as grey and hard as cold steel, as if searching for her soul. When finally he nodded, as if he had seen enough, she took an instinctive step back, unconsciously seeking the reassurance of her own roof-tree above her.

'What do you want?' she demanded.

'I came on Mary's behalf.' The measured control in his voice did nothing to disguise a tightening of the skin across the hard bones that moulded his cheeks. 'The doorstep is hardly appropriate in the circumstances.'

Sensing her resistance, he shrugged impatiently and took half a step back. 'If you wish, you may telephone that number from my car and verify my bona fides.'

'No. That won't be necessary.' She had no doubt that he was exactly who he said he was. No one bent on deception would make himself quite so unlikeable. Her reluctance to invite him in had more to do with a barely understood antagonism than fear. She did not want him in her home, but he clearly wasn't going anywhere until he had said whatever he had come to say. 'You'd better come in.'

Holly indicated the sitting-room

which had always seemed so warm and welcoming, but she looked at it now as Joshua Kent would see it. The worn patch on the carpet by the door, the shabby sofa, velvet curtains so old that the blue had faded to grey along the edges. Her home. Exactly as she liked it and he would just have to put up with it. But he didn't seem to notice his surroundings, his whole being intent only on her.

'Would you like some coffee?' she asked quickly, in an effort to distract him rather than from any belated desire to be hospitable. He refused, but took the chair she indicated.

Holly perched nervously on the sofa opposite him and waited. He sat forward in the slightly sagging armchair, his beautifully kept hands between his knees, long fingers meshed together. It seemed forever before he began but she waited. He had a force of presence that would make anyone wait to hear what he had to say.

'Mary died the night before last,'

he said at last, his voice warmer as he spoke her name. She realised then that for him Mary's death had been a real loss and wondered what exactly their relationship had been. Mary had been younger than her mother, or so it had appeared to her seven-year-old eyes.

Joshua Kent was more difficult to put an age to. There was a severity about him that made it difficult to judge how old he might be. But the smooth cap of hair was dense and black without a shadow of grey, and he moved, too, with that supple athletic grace of a man very much at the height of his powers, his full lower lip suggesting strong passions held, for the moment, by an iron self-control. If he smiled . . . Holly stopped the thought.

'I'm sorry,' she said, softening as she noticed dark smudges beneath his eyes that suggested a recent lack of sleep. 'What happened?'

'It was very sudden, a great shock to her friends, though I suspect not to Mary herself. Her affairs were left with the precision of someone who knows she won't have time for last-minute details.' He looked up then and any suggestion of warmth was obliterated by his frost-bitten expression. 'Except, apparently, for you.'

'Me?'

He nodded briefly. 'Her funeral is the day after tomorrow . . . '

A chill hand feathered her spine and Holly shuddered. Lilies, black hats, black cars and the mournful scent of damp earth and chrysanthemums.

'No.' Straight dark brows drew together in a frown and she realised she had spoken the word out loud. 'I'm sorry, Mr Kent,' she said as she realised how that must sound. 'I really cannot — '

'It was Mary's dying wish that you be present, Miss Carpenter. She made me promise to take you myself. That's why I'm here.' His mouth was drawn into a hard, uncompromising line. 'I have no intention of breaking that promise.'

Her dying wish? Holly's paint-smeared forehead creased slightly. 'But

I only met her once. Why . . . ?'

His look was pure disdain. 'Because she asked it of you. Isn't that enough?' He stood up. 'A small enough request in any circumstances. The bare minimum in these, I would have thought. However, I'll make it easy for you, Miss Carpenter.' He stared down at her. 'You are a beneficiary of her will and I am sure you will wish to be there to hear that document read after the service.' He ignored her gesture of protest. 'I'll pick you up here tomorrow morning at ten. Arrangements have been made for your accommodation. Afterwards — ' his lip curled derisively ' — should you wish to return here, I will make whatever arrangements you prefer.'

Holly leapt to her feet, stretching to every slender inch of her five feet seven. It did not feel nearly enough against the towering figure of Joshua Kent, but it would have to do. 'There will be absolutely no reason for you to make any arrangements for me. I have other plans for tomorrow.'

'Cancel them.'

He ignored her exclamation of outrage, merely allowing his gaze to drift up from the battered jeans, via the paint-covered smock, to meet her eyes head-on. 'Ashbrooke is a small town, rather conservative. Her friends will expect some token of mourning. I am authorised to advance you the money to buy something suitable.' He reached inside his jacket and began to extract notes from a soft leather wallet.

Holly's face darkened ominously. 'I have all the clothes I need, Mr Kent. Put your money away.'

His left eyebrow rose a fraction but, after a moment's hesitation, he replaced the wallet. 'What a very unusual woman you must be, Miss Carpenter.' He reached out and his fingers brushed so lightly over her forehead that she might have imagined the touch but for the immediate charge of electricity that made every nerve-ending leap frantically to attention. 'Let us hope they are the right ones. In the meantime, just make sure you wash your face and we'll get along fine. Until tomorrow at ten.'

She stood open-mouthed as he turned and walked through the door. In all her twenty-three years no one had ever spoken to her as this man had, left her feeling quite so small, so helpless in the face of his mind-numbing arrogance. He was half-way down the path before she regained the power to react, to make a move to stop him and let him know exactly what she thought of him and his outrageous demands.

'Wait!' she demanded from the door.

He paused, his hand on the gate and turned back, irritated to be delayed. 'Yes?'

She wanted to scream, put the hefty dent in so much arrogant effrontery, but some innate sense of self-preservation warned her that any attempt in that direction was doomed to failure.

'I'll send some flowers,' she offered.

'No flowers, by request.' There was a dreadful insistence about the man. 'Just you, Holly Carpenter. In person.'

'No,' she objected, almost desperately. 'I can't go with you. I have to work — '

'I'm sure that in the circumstances the college will be able to find a supply teacher to take your place,' he said. 'I'll telephone them myself if it will make things easier.'

She stared, for the moment speechless. He knew altogether too much about her and she didn't like it one bit. 'Who are you?' she demanded.

'You have my card. That tells you everything you need to know. Until ten o'clock tomorrow.'

'If I came . . . ' The cynical twist of his mouth, as he closed the gate behind him, told her that she had simply confirmed his worst suspicions. But why he should so obviously dislike her and what he suspected her of were not at all clear. He was already unlocking the door of his car and she advanced swiftly down the short path to the gate. 'If I came, I would prefer to make my own way to Ashbrooke, Mr Kent.'

He looked over the roof of the car

at her. 'I'm sure you would, Miss Carpenter. But since you have no idea where the funeral is to be held or the will read . . . ' his pause was just long enough to be insulting ' . . . you'll just have to put up with my company. And this way I'll be certain you won't change your mind.'

He didn't wait for her agreement or otherwise, but ducked into the car and a minute later might never have been there at all. Except that her pulse was beating an angry tattoo in her throat and when she looked down her hands were clenched into small fists, the knuckles white. She slowly opened them, the effort of extending her fingers almost painful. Then she turned and walked stiffly back into the house.

She paused and drew a sharp breath as she caught sight of herself in the hall mirror, shaken by the vivid, angry patches of colour that stood out against the pallor of her skin. If Joshua Kent had taken away that impression of her it was no surprise that he had looked so contemptuous. With her cheeks aflame and her hair tied back under a scarf she looked like some half-mad gypsy from a Victorian melodrama.

She snatched off the scarf that covered her hair to keep it from the paint and the thick, soft mane, silver-gilt in the afternoon light filtering through the glass door, swung about her cheeks. The hectic colour was already beginning to fade, leaving just a gentle flush to mould the fine bones and set off the spark he had provoked to darken her eyes.

She shrugged. What did it matter? She went back to the conservatory that she used as a studio and where she had been working when she had been interrupted by the urgent summons of the bell. She had been struggling with the picture all afternoon, but now, seeing it afresh, she saw exactly what she must do.

She swished her brush furiously through the water and stroked it across the colour, determined to put the disturbing Joshua Kent and his equally disturbing errand out of her mind entirely and carry on with her work. But her hand shook as she touched the paper and the brush jabbed out of control.

Holly sighed and blotted at the paper with a rag in an effort to minimise the damage, but somehow it no longer mattered. The delicate little water-colour had been destined along with half-a-dozen others for the small gallery in the High Street that was a favourite haunt of summer visitors to the picturesque Thameside town.

They would have taken many more, but she had refused to be seduced by the easy money to be made by churning out pretty postcard scenes. Except now, because her ancient car had required a hundred and fifty pounds spent on it just to keep it going, she had needed the extra money for her Easter holiday visiting the galleries in Florence and this had been the only way.

Joshua Kent had said she was a

beneficiary of Mary's will. She allowed herself briefly to dwell on the fantasy of having enough money to give up working and just concentrate on painting. Then the faces of her students intruded, all ages and abilities, with only one thing in common — the desperate longing to paint.

Furious with herself, she took the picture and rent it in two. She felt restored by the action, almost as if it were Joshua Kent's immaculate white shirt-front she had torn and held in rags between her fingers. There was an unexpected satisfaction in the thought. Then she looked down at the paper in her hands and shook her head. 'Stupid,' she said softly.

She was allowing his visit to upset her and that was ridiculous. His manner had been disturbing, it was true. No one had ever really disapproved of her before. But, no matter what Mr high-and-mighty Kent thought, she wouldn't be tempted into attending a funeral because of any bequest. It would almost certainly be nothing more than some small token — a trinket left to her in deference to her mother.

She crushed the paper between her fingers and dropped it in the bin, then gathered up her brushes and began to wash them. Besides, she knew from experience that a funeral would upset her for days.

But it was odd how clearly she remembered the eager, anxious face bending over her as a child, hoping she would like the doll she had brought her. She remembered, too, the tears hurriedly blinked back by her mother and her own guilt at wanting the doll so very much that she had pushed the strange woman away and run to her mother's arms.

How had she looked, Mary Graham, lying on her hospital bed, begging Joshua Kent to make sure that Holly came to her funeral? An over-vivid imagination supplied the answer. If she went with him, it wouldn't be because he demanded that she should. It would be because . . . She shook the water from her brushes and stuck them, too fiercely, in a pot to dry. It toppled and fell to the hard quarry-tile floor and smashed in a thousand pieces.

'Oh! Bother!' Joshua Kent's visit had unsettled her more than she had been prepared to admit. The memory of Mary's visit had been deep-buried and her mother had never spoken of it, or Mary Graham, again. And the doll had been put away.

She cleared up the mess, taking excessive care to hunt for every last shard of glass, wrapping it carefully in newspaper before putting it in the bin. She found another pot for her brushes, tidied her paints, straightened her easel . . . stalled endlessly.

It was only when there was nothing left to stay the moment that she climbed the stairs to the little room that had been hers for as long as she could remember.

It hadn't changed much. The wall-paper was still the same daisy pattern that her father had put up the year before he died. It was scuffed now, bumped by furniture and marked by drawing-pins from teenage posters. She knew she ought to redecorate it, but there were so many other expenses in an old house.

The decision to share it, to let one of her spare bedrooms, had been made six months earlier in an effort to defray some of the costs. She had been putting off the evil moment, but she was going to have to face the prospect of letting the other bedroom. The only alternative was working extra hours, but the talk in the common-room was all of cut-backs, not expansion. Still, she would leave the final decision until after her holiday.

She opened the cupboard door. There was a neat stack of favourite childhood books that she couldn't bear to part with, a collection of shells. The costume dolls that her father had brought her back from his trips abroad filled the centre shelf.

But the doll she had come to find wasn't there. It was at the bottom, buried under a sleeping-bag and rucksack, but after a moment's search she found it, picked it up and held it at arm's length.

It was a very superior sort of rag doll, from a London store. The material still had that new, starchy smell; the lace edges of the dress and bonnet were still crisp. Little fingers had never disturbed her pristine condition or loved her to a state of tattiness. Only very occasionally had Holly taken her from her hiding place and held her, to show the doll that she did love her, but couldn't ever let her mother see.

Now Joshua Kent had come, disturbing memories she thought she had forgotten. Disturbing her with his arrogant, dictatorial manner. He had obviously been irritated because she hadn't immediately agreed to his demand. But it had been far more than that. He hadn't wanted to come at all. In fact, despite his determination that she comply with Mary's wishes, she was almost certain that he didn't want her anywhere near Ashbrooke. And that fact alone might be enough to take her there.

2

Despite the luxury of the car, it was an uncomfortable journey. Holly had been prepared to make the best of things, try to get along, but from the moment she'd opened the door to Joshua Kent's summons on the bell at precisely ten o'clock it had been apparent that the antagonism was as fierce as ever.

She had stood perfectly still for a moment, while he had run an assessing eye over her long, narrow grey coat and the soft-brimmed black velvet hat she wore pulled down over her forehead.

'Will I do?' she had asked finally, masking the slow burn of anger beneath the cool tones of her voice.

'Perfectly,' he had acknowledged briefly, with a slight, knowing twist to his mouth as he took her bag and headed for the car. He'd opened the door for her and, with the utmost reluctance, she'd got in. He'd climbed in beside her and once again subjected her to the scrutiny of a pair of steely eyes. 'You've obviously taken a great deal of trouble with your appearance,' he'd said. 'Wasted on me, of course, but Mary's friends will no doubt appreciate your efforts.'

Holly could hardly believe her ears. 'How dare you speak to me like that?' she'd exclaimed. 'You are quite insufferable.' She had turned to open the door, determined now that whatever happened she was not going to spend the journey to Ashbrooke cooped up with this man.

The click of the central-locking system had forestalled her and she had turned on him to protest, but one look at the severe lines of his face had told her that there would be no point and she'd refrained from telling him exactly what she thought of him. The journey would be unpleasant enough in the circumstances.

He had smiled slightly in appreciation

of her restraint. 'Sorry, Miss Carpenter. I'm afraid for the moment you'll just have to suffer.'

'Why?' she'd demanded.

'I suggest that you address that question to your conscience,' he'd replied tersely. He had glanced over his shoulder and pulled away from the kerb, apparently expecting no answer and getting none. Holly was completely mystified by his attitude to her, but, since he had made it quite plain that he was not going to offer an explanation, had contented herself with keeping her eyes on the passing countryside and trying to pretend that he wasn't there.

But it was difficult. All the time she was edgily aware of the brooding presence beside her and she found herself pondering on the coldness of his manner towards her. No one, in all her twenty-three years of existence, had ever spoken to her as he had. She wanted to grab his shoulders and shake him, demand an answer. She glanced at him and, despite her buttoned-down fury, almost smiled at the thought. As if she would make any impression on the pair of hard, square shoulders that filled the well-padded seat of the Rolls.

And in a way, she acknowledged, he was right about her appearance. She had dressed for a funeral, perhaps wanting to impress him with her sincerity. Some hopes! His own appearance had been far more casual than her own: dark trousers, an open-necked shirt and a russet cashmere sweater that lent a little of its warmth to his eyes, and she was sure that he was a great deal more comfortable than she was in her close-fitting coat. She was tempted to remove her hat, but a certain stubborn pride made her cling to it.

As if sensing her inspection he glanced at her, staring down his long, straight nose, and their eyes met. A slight frown creased his forehead as if she had momentarily jolted that imperious assurance. Then he turned back to the road and his hard profile told her nothing. And that suited her, Holly told herself. She had no desire to know anything about the man. And she promised herself that she would be getting a train home.

She still didn't quite understand the impulse that was taking her to Ashbrooke. She had lain awake half the night, determined that she wouldn't go anywhere with Joshua Kent, and had found herself wondering if he would simply pick her up and carry her off. She wouldn't have put it past him.

She had approached her head of department confident that the imminent end of term would make taking time off impossible. But Harvey had been primed and couldn't have been more sympathetic.

'Mr Kent telephoned this afternoon. He said you were under the impression that it would be impossible for you to take time off to go to your cousin's funeral.' He'd tutted. 'I thought you knew me better than that, Holly. Of course you must go, and don't worry about rushing back for the last couple of days of term. I'm sure there will be all sorts of things you need to do. We'll see you at the beginning of the summer. Give my regards to Florence.' He grinned. 'Though I don't suppose she'll remember me.'

Holly had laughed automatically at his joke, but underneath she had boiled. How dared Joshua Kent presume to interfere in her life? And why couldn't Harvey have been a little tougher, instead of the kindest man in the college?

David's attitude had been rather more mercenary. 'You'd better go, Holly,' he'd said as he prepared to leave for work. 'The old dear might have left you a few thousand.'

'There's no reason why she should,' Holly had snapped, 'and she wasn't old.' As a lodger David Grantham was fine, she'd thought crossly, sorting through her wardrobe for something suitable to wear. As a human being? She had occasional moments of doubt about him on that score.

When she had decided to share the house, in an effort to cut down the running costs, a friend had advised her to take in a man. Someone who could mend fuses, clear the guttering and put up shelves when occasion demanded.

She hadn't taken the advice seriously — she was perfectly capable of doing all those things herself — but David had answered her ad, taking advantage of his job on the local newspaper to get in before she was inundated with other applicants.

They had discovered they had met once before when he had written a feature about her for the local paper; he was easy to get along with and in the main it had worked well enough.

She sighed and stared out of the car window. They had already left the motorway far behind and Holly tried to concentrate on the countryside. She had never been to Devon before and she was surprised how advanced everything was. The hedgerow was already beginning to quicken with life, with occasional dark patches of violets amid the gaudy celandines. Then she caught sight of a rabbit bounding panic-stricken along the road, and cried out a warning.

'I've seen it,' Joshua said sharply, slowing until the creature dived into the safety of the hedge.

'I've never seen a wild rabbit before,' she said, feeling a little foolish.

'You'll see plenty about here. They're pests.'

'In that case,' she retorted, 'I'm surprised that you didn't simply run it over.'

'Perhaps, Miss Carpenter, I'm not blessed with your ruthless streak,' he said smoothly.

'Don't underestimate yourself, Mr Kent.'

He threw her a venomous glance and then slipped a CD into the car's stereo system. Mozart flooded the sound vacuum, indicating in no uncertain terms that conversation was at an end.

Half an hour later she caught her first

glimpse of the sea as the hills dipped away and an involuntary exclamation of pleasure escaped her lips.

'Do you like the sea?' The totally unexpected sound of his voice made her jump.

'Yes,' she admitted, oddly reluctant even to grant him this small insight into her thoughts.

A slight tightening of his lips might almost have been a smile. 'How fortunate.'

'Fortunate?' It seemed an odd choice of words. 'I don't see how. This isn't exactly a treat for me.'

'Isn't it?'

She turned quickly, hardly believing her ears. 'What did you say?'

'It's all right, Miss Carpenter. There's no need to pretend with me. I know who you are. Why you're here. You can keep the act for those who'll appreciate it.'

'Do you, Mr Kent?' Her voice mocked him. 'I know why I'm here when I'd rather be almost anywhere else in the whole world.' Because, despite her horror of funerals, and despite everything Joshua Kent might think, in the end she had known that she would never forgive herself if she didn't pay her last respects to Mary Graham. 'But I'd bet a hundred pounds that you haven't a clue.'

'If you had a hundred pounds to bet,' he said, 'I would take you up on that.' Before she could think of a suitable response he had slowed to turn through a pair of ornate gates, driving her half a mile or so before pulling up in front of a fine three-storey building. 'I've booked you in at Ashbrooke Hall. It used to be a country house,' he said, glancing up at the façade. 'But now it's a hotel. I think you'll find it comfortable.'

Holly was horrified. The cost of a night in such a place would take her a month to earn. At least.

'I can't stay here,' she protested. But he was already out of the car and her bag was being borne away by a porter. He opened her door and Holly climbed out. 'Please!' She put a hand on his arm, determined to make him see.

He glanced down at the long, narrow fingers pale against his sweater and relented slightly. 'No one expects you to pay, Miss Carpenter. It is an expense on the estate — '

She stiffened and pulled her hand away. 'I don't want to be an expense to anyone. Just take me somewhere ordinary and I'll be happy to pay my own hotel bill . . . ' Her voice trailed off as she saw the view that stretched away beneath them. An old harbour, sheltered against the wind by a long breakwater, a mixture of ocean-going yachts and more workmanlike craft riding on the high tide. Spreading up the hill towards them were all kinds of dwellings. White-painted cottages near the quay, the huddle of the town itself and then the more substantial properties perched higher to enjoy the full impact of the rugged coastline that rose around the gentle sandy sweep of the bay.

'It's beautiful,' she said.

He had no eyes for the view. 'Mary wanted your stay, however brief, to be as pleasant as possible in the circumstances.'

The hours of self-restraint, while confined with this unbearable man, had taken their toll and she snapped. 'What a pity she didn't think of that when she sent you to fetch me!'

'You little — ' He broke off. 'I ought to tan your backside.'

'Here?' she demanded. 'In front of all these people?'

His face darkened momentarily. 'It'll keep.' And, apparently contented at the startled widening of her amber eyes, he took her firmly by the arm and urged her forward. 'We'll go inside if you've stopped making a show of protesting.' She bit down hard and for a moment resisted, her low heels digging into the gravel, but his eyes dared her to make a scene in front of a party of guests gathered in the entrance and watching their arrival with interest.

He swiftly dealt with the formalities

of registration, giving her a moment to catch her breath and recover from the scene in the drive.

'I'll take you up.'

'There's no need,' she said, quickly, 'I can manage . . .'

A trace of a smile crossed his features as he saw her nervous reaction. 'I said it'll keep, Miss Carpenter. I don't lie.'

'Just beat on helpless women?'

'Helpless? Hardly that. Not while you've a tongue in your head.' He didn't wait for her response, but turned and led the way to the room that had been allocated to her on the first floor. It quite took her breath away. It must have been one of the main chambers of the house, the luxurious furnishings dominated by a richly hung four-poster bed and, despite the brightness of the spring day, a fire burned in a stone hearth.

But it was the view that enthralled Holly and she walked quickly across to the window. The gardens were full of spring flowers far in advance of those at home, and the glimpse of the sea beyond made her fingers itch for her sketchpad.

'Oh, this is so beautiful.' She couldn't wait to throw off the formal clothes that she had worn just to show him and get outside . . . She pulled off her hat and shook her fair, shoulder-length hair loose. There was a squirrel in the garden raiding a bird table and it had just managed to detach half a coconut and was escaping with it in its mouth. 'Just look at that.' She laughed and turned, wanting to share the moment, but he was staring at her, his face rigid with disbelief. 'What is it?' She impulsively put her hand to her forehead, wondering if the smear of paint had somehow reappeared there.

'I . . . ' He shook his head. 'Nothing.' His voice was clipped. 'I have things to do. Can you look after yourself for the rest of the day?'

'I look after myself every day, Mr Kent,' she said without rancour, more interested in the sudden glimpse of a human being behind the cold mask. 'I'm sure I can fill in a few hours without someone to hold my hand.'

He nodded and walked quickly to the door. 'I'll join you here for dinner.' He half turned to her. 'Eight o'clock.' He didn't wait for her answer; apparently it was unthinkable that she might refuse his company. Instead he strode away on long legs that carried him out of the door and down the stairs before she had time to collect her wits and tell him that she didn't need anyone to make certain she used the correct knife.

But the day was too pretty to waste on such pettiness. She would worry about Joshua Kent at eight o'clock, she promised herself, not a moment before. She quickly unpacked and changed into a pair of navy trousers and a warm turquoise sweater. Then, taking the leather folder that contained her sketch-pad and pastels, she made her way down into the garden. Settling herself on a bench that might have been placed there especially for her purpose, Holly opened the pad and began to sketch an outline of the view.

But she found that it wasn't quite so simple to dismiss Joshua Kent from her mind. His cynical expression continually inserted itself between her and the block of paper, destroying her attempts at concentration. The effort of capturing the important lines of a distant scene would normally be sufficient to hold her, drive everything else from her head. But today the only lines she could see clearly were the arrogant tilt of his head, the straight line of his nose and the hard, disapproving mouth.

Her hand moved in swift, angry strokes over the paper and in seconds a caricature of Joshua Kent sneered back at her, the exaggerated curve of his lower lip a sensual counterpoint to her savage portrayal of the man.

Holly stared in horror at what she had done. At college her caricatures were always in demand for special occasions and newsletters, and she had drawn them of students and lecturers alike with humour and affection. But this was something deeper; it was very personal and the intensity of it almost scared her.

What on earth was it about him that brought out the very worst in her? It was as if from the moment she had opened the door to his imperious ring some basic instinct had sent up a warning signal that he was trouble and she must be on her guard.

Tentatively, almost reluctantly, her finger traced the lines she had drawn. It was a cruel portrait. And not quite true. It missed something she had glimpsed, very briefly, in that moment she had turned from the window. Something he was taking great pains to hide from her.

Holly shivered convulsively. She didn't know why she had come to Ashbrooke. Why he had insisted that she come. But it had to be more than a childhood memory of a pretty face blanked with pain that she had somehow caused.

★　★　★

He was prompt, but she hadn't expected anything else. She hadn't packed anything very grand — she didn't have anything grand to pack — but she had twisted her hair up into a smooth chignon and her dark blue dress had a classic simplicity that would take it to most places without raising an eyebrow. However, it was clearly not up to the dining-room at Ashbrooke Hall.

'You'd better bring a coat. We'll go to a restaurant in the town, rather than eat here. It'll be quieter.'

'If you'd prefer not to be seen with me, Mr Kent, just say so. I would be perfectly happy with something on a tray in my room.'

Her comment apparently hit the mark. 'It's nothing to do with your appearance. You look . . . charming.'

Holly wondered why it had hurt him so much to say that. It had almost been torn from him. She opened her wardrobe and took out her grey coat. When she turned back he was idly turning the pages of her sketchpad.

'No . . . ' She took half a step towards him, but it was too late.

He stared at the appalling caricature. She held her breath, but there was no reaction. No exclamation of rage. Nothing. He simply closed the pad and looked up at her. 'Ready? Then we'll go.'

It was a quite terrifying demonstration of self-control and she was still holding her breath as they walked through Reception, expecting a delayed eruption. But fate was kind.

'Joshua, darling, you're home.' A dark-haired beauty kissed his cheek and looked as if she would have liked to do considerably more if the place had been less public and her husband had not been only a few steps behind. 'How long are you staying?'

He glanced at the man behind her. 'Just a few days.'

'Back for Mary's funeral?' The man didn't wait for an answer but turned to Holly and eyed her with interest. 'And who's this?'

'Holly Carpenter. Lisa and Brian Stamford.' The introduction was brief almost to the point of rudeness. 'Holly was Mary's cousin,' he added, as if he found it necessary to explain why he was with her. Holly had not missed the hungry expression in the woman's eyes.

'Why don't you join us for dinner?' Lisa suggested hopefully.

But Brian unexpectedly intervened. 'Don't be silly, Lisa. The girl won't want to be dancing the night before the funeral of her — ' he glanced enquiringly at the other man ' — cousin, did you say?' Joshua nodded. Brian Stamford regarded her for a moment, then shook his head. 'Astonishing.' He turned back to Lisa. 'Josh will be taking her somewhere quiet.'

'The Ship,' Joshua confirmed.

Brian nodded. 'Good food. You'll enjoy it,' he added for Holly's benefit, and patted her hand. 'My condolences to you, m'dear. We'll see you tomorrow.' They headed for the dining-room.

'Shall we go?' Joshua prompted.

Feeling about six inches tall, Holly

knew that, no matter how much it might stick in her throat, she had to apologise to the man. She hadn't known Mary, but he had and she doubted very much if he felt like dancing or even eating in such an atmosphere. 'I'm sorry, Mr Kent. I didn't realise.'

'There's no reason why you should know that the Hall has a regular dinner-dance on Wednesday evenings,' he said rather brusquely. Then he unbent sufficiently to say, 'I'd prefer it if you called me Joshua.'

If Holly thought this tokened a thaw in his attitude to her she was quickly disabused of any such notion.

He was grimly quiet in the car and at the restaurant they were ushered to a seat as far from public view as possible, which she thought was taking things a little bit far. Not that she was prepared to say so.

She was too aware of some strong emotion, firmly suppressed for the moment, but still smouldering danger- ously just below the chill mask of civility, and she was glad to take refuge behind the menu.

But the words made no impression on her. If only she knew why he was so antagonistic towards her. She had just about screwed herself up to the point of demanding to know what she had done to make him dislike her so much, when his voice cut across her thoughts.

'Have you made a decision? Or do you need a little longer?'

'I'm sorry,' she said, making an effort to pull herself together. 'I was thinking — '

'Were you? You have my sympathy.' His voice, heavy with irony, made her look up. 'Your thoughts cannot be very comfortable to live with right now.'

Her temper flared. 'I was thinking about you, Mr Kent. I leave you to make your own decision as to how enjoyable an exercise that might be.'

'I see,' he said.

'I doubt it. It would be quite impossible for someone with your insufferable arrogance to understand

43

quite how unbearable your behaviour has been.'

She glanced quickly at the menu and chose the first thing that she saw. It hardly mattered what it was. Her appetite was practically non-existent and the sooner she could get back to the privacy of her room, the better she would like it.

He summoned the waiter to give him their order and then sat back in his chair, his eyes firmly fixed on her. 'Mary told me that you're a painter.'

'You talked about me?'

'It seemed to help her. You were on her mind a great deal at the end.' His mouth tightened, but he was apparently making some sort of effort to be civil, so perhaps her words had struck a nerve. 'It was quite reasonable of her to take an interest, surely? Are you any good?'

She wasn't used to people asking her to pass judgement on her own work and, confused by his constant switching of attack, she hardly knew what to say.

'I paint pictures that people like. They buy them, anyway. Water-colours, mostly.'

'Pretty landscapes?' he suggested, making no attempt to conceal his contempt.

She reflected on the series she had almost finished for the gallery. Bread-and-butter pictures in the main and she acknowledged that there was some truth in his remark, no matter how much it hurt. 'If you like. But I do other things.'

'Well, you'll find plenty around here to paint.'

'I tried this afternoon. But I'm afraid I couldn't concentrate.'

'Yes,' he said a little drily. 'I noticed. You don't confine yourself entirely to landscapes.' She was thankful that the lighting was dim enough to hide the shaming flush that darkened her cheeks.

'No, not entirely,' she confessed, then, desperate to turn the conversation to less dangerous subjects, she asked, 'Do you live in Ashbrooke, Mr Kent?'

'Yes, when I'm not in London. I own Ashbrooke Hall.'

'Ashbrooke Hall?' She was stunned.

'I hadn't realised — you hardly seem . . .'

'The type to run a hotel?' he finished for her. He twirled the stem of his glass. 'I'm not. I don't. And I thought I'd asked you to call me Joshua?' He shrugged. 'It was my family home. By the time my sisters were married and it was just my father and I rattling around in it like a couple of bones it seemed a bit pointless.'

'But it's lovely,' she protested.

'Yes. It is.' His mouth twisted into something that might have been a smile. 'It would be dreadfully selfish to keep it all to myself, don't you think?'

She acknowledged his smile. 'How very altruistic of you, Mr Kent. Joshua,' she corrected herself.

'Do you think so, Holly?' he said, stressing her name, and she almost thought he might be making fun of her. But that seemed highly unlikely. 'It's just good business. My father wanted to live in France so I bought him out and leased the place to an Italian hotelier who was looking for a base to launch himself in England.'

'Only leased?' she asked.

'At the time I couldn't quite bring myself to let it go entirely.'

'But now you can?' Because Mary was dead? Had they been that close?

'Frankly, it makes a much better hotel. It's been a great success and Luigi is anxious to make the arrangement permanent. Perhaps it is the right time to cut myself loose.'

'That sounds a little sad.'

'Sad?' He considered the matter for a moment. 'The end of an era perhaps. And no bad thing. Those sort of houses were fine when you could employ armies of cheap labour to run them.'

'If you weren't part of the army,' she pointed out.

'If you weren't part of the army,' he agreed, with a sudden smile. 'And meanwhile you, Holly, have the pleasure of sleeping in my four-poster bed.'

'Your bed?' The image of his dark head against the lace-edged pillow, the broad shoulders, a naked chest sprinkled with dark hair revealed as he threw back the cover to invite her in brought a slow burn to her cheeks, exposing her to his ridicule.

'Does that bother you?' he asked.

'No,' she said quickly. 'Why should it?'

'No reason. But I would have thought an enquiry as to whether I was still using it before you answered in the negative was advisable. Or maybe you're not that fussy.' He looked up. 'Ah, here's our dinner at last.'

Relief at the interruption to the conversation was so overwhelming that she left his last query unchallenged. But when, on their return to the hotel, he insisted on seeing her to her room she began to feel a little nervous. His hand at her back was possessive; he was at home here, master of all he surveyed. He unlocked the door and stood back to let her enter.

She turned abruptly in the doorway. 'Goodnight, Joshua. Thank you for dinner.'

'I think I can safely claim that the pleasure was all mine, Holly.' He handed her the key. 'Better make sure you lock your door.'

He stepped back and she shut the door and turned the key. She then had the humiliation of hearing him laughing all the way down the corridor. 'Hateful man,' she said. But she spent the night imagining that the room smelt faintly of something indefinable that was Joshua Kent.

* * *

Holly had been certain that it would rain. Funerals were linked in her mind with rain. But the sun was shining as Joshua parked outside the little grey stone church.

It was already crowded with people and she was conscious of a great many eyes on her as he introduced her to the vicar, then led her up the aisle of the church to her seat in the front pew. She wanted to protest that it wasn't her place, but it was hardly the time to make a fuss, so she slid on to the ancient seat and he sat alongside her and handed her the order of the service, and she was glad, despite everything, to have his strength at her side as the occasion threatened to overwhelm her.

Afterwards Mary's friends crowded into her pretty cream and pink drawing-room for tea. All the while Joshua kept close to her elbow, fielding the intense smalltown curiosity about the stranger, introducing her again and again as, 'Holly Carpenter, Mary's cousin . . . ' as if it was somehow important to stress the relationship.

At least the constant need to shake hands and smile kept at bay the unhappy memories of her mother's funeral on the cold, wet Christmas Eve that had been her twenty-first birthday. Finally, though, people began to drift away and Joshua, who had momentarily disappeared, was at her side.

'Marcus wants you in the study now, Holly.' He ushered her across the hall into the small study where Mary's solicitor had already settled himself and arranged his papers. She had already been introduced to Mary's solicitor, Marcus Lynton, and he looked up and smiled.

'Sit down, Miss Carpenter, Joshua. This won't take long.' He looked over his spectacles at the pair of them, and when he was satisfied that he had their undivided attention he began to read the last will and testament of Mary Elizabeth Graham.

As she listened, Holly felt more and more confused. Her glance involuntarily flickered across the room to the stony figure of Joshua Kent, expecting him every moment to leap up and announce that he would be contesting every line of Mary Graham's will. But presumably he already knew its contents. In any event he said nothing, but the stiff disapproval of his features spoke volumes.

'It will take a week or two for all the formalities to be settled.' The solicitor's voice broke into her thoughts. 'But you won't have to bother about any of that. Joshua, as executor, will deal with everything for you,' he said, under the mistaken impression that this information would reassure her. 'Naturally, you will have access to whatever sum you need for your immediate use. As for the house, you will no doubt wish to take advice about selling it. Unless of course,' he went on, 'you plan to move to Ashbrooke? It is a charming place to live and this is a delightful house.' The man's smile was unforced. He at least had no trouble with the disposal of Mary's estate. He seemed to expect some sort of answer, but Holly was too stunned to think of anything sensible to say.

'I'm sure Miss Carpenter has no wish to move away from all her friends.' She felt Joshua Kent's cool grey eyes on her. They were quite clearly daring her to attempt to live in Mary's house, or in any way take her place.

'Well, there's no hurry. Show her

round, Joshua. Convince her we're not all old fogies and that she would be very welcome.'

'I really couldn't put Mr Kent to so much trouble,' Holly said quickly, glancing across at him. For a second their eyes clashed.

'It's no trouble. You should see everything before you make up your mind.' His smooth voice did not fool her for a minute, but the solicitor was already taking her hand and assuring her that he would be happy to give her any assistance she needed. Joshua Kent shut the door behind the man and turned to her.

'So, where would you like to start?' he asked. 'Down here, or upstairs?'

'Start?'

'Well, you won't want to waste any time assessing your new-found wealth. That is what you came for, after all.'

She was still trying to come to terms with what she had just been told — that, apart from bequests to friends and employees, and a sum to set up a

53

trust for a local charity that she had helped found, Mary Graham had left her entire estate to her closest living relative, Holly Carpenter. Her house, all her personal possessions and what to Holly seemed like a fortune.

'I thought she had left me some keepsake because of my mother. They were cousins, but you must have known that . . . a brooch or something.'

'Ashbrooke is a long way to come for a brooch, Holly. 'Something', however, is rather different.'

Her head jerked back at the hardness in his voice. 'I came because she asked; you told me she asked — '

'Yes, I did. But you were distinctly reluctant to put in an appearance until I mentioned a bequest.'

'That wasn't the reason — '

'No?'

'No, Joshua Kent, but, since you made it more than clear when you came to my house that you were predisposed to believe the very worst of me, I will not even bother to challenge that view.'

'Very wise.'

She was close to tears, but she wasn't about to let this hateful man see how he had managed to upset her. She had the feeling he would like that. She walked away while she fought the sting against her eyelids. Then she straightened and turned to face him. 'I didn't know Mary. I don't know why she left me all this, but I'm glad she did. It would be hypocritical of me to pretend otherwise.'

'Something like winning the football pools, but without the bother of filling in the coupon?' he suggested.

'If that's what you choose to think, there's no point in attempting to explain how I feel. But I refuse to don sackcloth and ashes just to satisfy your sense of what's proper — '

'Why not? You did a first-class job with your appearance for the funeral. The grieving relative. So young, so beautiful. Quite a performance.'

She stared at him, shocked by his open bitterness.

'It wasn't — '

'Shall we begin?' he interrupted. He wasn't interested in anything she had to say, was the unmistakable message, and she gave up any attempt to convince him that she wasn't the mercenary little tramp he so clearly thought her. What did it matter, after all? She knew what she was and after everything was settled she would never have to see Joshua Kent again. Except that he was Mary's executor and would no doubt be around for some time. But not now. She didn't have to take any more of his unpleasantness now.

'You needn't stay, Joshua. I would much prefer to look around my house on my own,' she said. She took some satisfaction at the whiteness that appeared around his mouth. He wasn't the only one who could wound with his tongue. 'That is what the solicitor said? There's no misunderstanding? It is my house now?' She persisted in driving the point home.

'There was no misunderstanding. In fact, you seem to have a very firm grasp of the situation.' He took a step towards her. 'Can you wait until tomorrow before seeing the estate agent? Or are you in a real hurry to get your hands on the money? What a pity we let Brian Stamford go, but I'm sure he would be more than willing to come back straight away and start measuring up — '

It was the last straw and she snapped. It had been a difficult day and her total confusion on learning she was Mary's heir had not made it any easier. She no longer cared what Joshua Kent thought about her. Her sole intent was to leave him in no doubt as to how she felt about him.

'What is it with you, Joshua Kent? Does it offend you so much that Mary left her beautiful house and all her money to one of the great unwashed? Someone you've decided, for no good reason that I am aware of, is totally unworthy?' She made a reckless move towards him. 'Or is it rather more personal than that?' Her eyes sparked with a fury unleashed by the constant pin-pricks of his resentment. A resentment she thought she was beginning to understand. 'Could it be,' she demanded, ignoring the angry compression of his mouth, the glacial expression in his eyes, 'could it just be that you believed she would leave all this to you?'

3

Joshua Kent's fingers bit into Holly's arm as he reached out and hauled her close, cutting off the flow of invective as effectively as if he had her by the throat.

'That's enough!' For a moment they stood, chest to chest, defying one another in a dizzying clash of wills. Then, without warning, he released her and she staggered back, rubbing the feeling back into her arm where he had gripped her. 'Mary was a very dear friend. She deserves better than you for a . . . ' He stopped himself with enormous effort. 'But I made her a promise and, by God, I'll keep it, in spite of you. However, right now I've had just about all I can take, so I'll leave you to an assessment of your gains.' His sweeping gesture took in the house. 'How long do you think it will take? An hour? Longer perhaps?' He didn't wait for her answer. 'I'll collect you at six-thirty.'

White-faced, trembling under this latest onslaught, she hit back. 'Don't bother. I'll call a taxi. After all, I should be able to afford it now.' For a moment time held its breath. Then, with a visible effort of will, Joshua Kent stepped back.

'Indeed you should. In fact, you could call a whole rank of taxis if the mood were to take you. But you won't, Holly. We'll play out this charade to the bitter end. I'll be back.' He turned and left, very quietly, his self-control screwed tightly back in place.

Holly let out a long sigh of relief. She had not misjudged the battened-down passion she had read in his face. Released, in love or hate, its force would be devastating. She rubbed again at the place where his fingers had gripped her and allowed herself a rueful smile. There was no doubt which of those particular passions he reserved for her.

But why he should hate her was as much a mystery as ever and as bewildering. Her easygoing nature had never roused anyone to such strong passion before. Of either variety. Standing alone in the sitting-room of Mary's house, Holly shivered slightly and wondered if perhaps love at first sight had a contrary and equally violent emotion.

She looked around her. While they had been closeted with the solicitor, the caterers had cleared everything away. No sign remained that anything unusual had taken place. She wandered over to the window and stared out. It was nearly dark now. Too late to look at the garden. She had caught just a glimpse as they had driven through the gate, seen the brave sweep of daffodils that curved down the driveway.

And yet she was reluctant to look around the house. She had only said that that was her intention to annoy Joshua Kent. Now she found herself almost wishing that she had not asked him to leave. With him as her guide it would not have felt quite so much like snooping on someone else's life. But she supposed if she was going home the next day it must be done. Although exactly why, what she was doing it for, she couldn't have said.

She wandered from room to room, touching the delicate china pieces that were lodged almost carelessly on window-ledges and small tables. Not like her mother's precious pieces, locked out of harm's way in a china cabinet. But there had been no careless children or tail-wagging dogs here to keep them locked away from. Mary Graham had apparently led a very self-contained life.

Upstairs, the bedrooms were all quite beautiful, freshly decorated, in stunning contrast to her own shabby room at home, everything in perfect order. The housekeeper knew her business. They had met briefly after the funeral when Joshua had introduced her to Mrs Austin. The woman had looked at her closely, in a manner Holly had found

62

slightly disconcerting. Now she knew why. The poor lady was clearly wondering what sort of person had inherited the house and whether she would still have a job.

Mary's bedroom was at the front and in the daytime would have the sea views. Holly could see the lights of the harbour and the town and, a long way off, in the shipping lanes, the tiny moving lights of tankers and cargo boats.

This room, too, had an almost unnatural perfection, except that on the bed there was a battered manila folder. It was so out of place among the broderie frills that she picked it up. She flipped it open and all at once the breath caught in her throat.

There was a photograph. An old photograph of herself, grinning, gaptoothed, pleased as punch to be big enough to go to school, white-blonde hair pulled back in tight pigtails, beret firmly in place at the regulation angle, posed to show the badge on the tiny blazer pocket. She picked it up. A copy of the picture had had pride of place on the mantelpiece at home until it had been knocked over in some mad game and the glass had broken. She sank to the bed and began slowly to turn the rest of the papers over.

'Holly?' She hadn't been aware of time passing, but now the sound of her name jerked her back to the present.

'Oh, Joshua.' She was slightly dazed. 'Is it so late? I hadn't realised.'

He came into the room and stood beside her. 'I'm sorry, I didn't mean you to find that cold. Mary asked me to give it to you.'

He picked up the yellowing cutting from the local newspaper when she'd won her first painting competition. 'You were a fragile little thing,' he said. 'Is this the card?' She nodded. She had been six and still remembered the thrill when they had used her picture for a Christmas card to raise money for a local charity. He opened it and read out her very careful 'With love from Holly'.

A choked cry escaped her lips. 'I didn't know about this,' she said. 'Why did Mary have all these things?'

He frowned and sat beside her on the bed and began sifting through the papers. Copies of school reports, more newspaper cuttings of her successes.

'Good grief!' She looked up at his exclamation and he held out a newspaper cutting.

'Oh, no!' She saw the question in his face and managed a laugh. 'My moment of teenage rebellion,' she offered. A punk hairdo. It had unhappily coincided with one of her paintings being chosen for a national exhibition. 'My mother was so angry.'

He hesitated. 'She has my sympathy.' He reached out and touched her hair with the tips of his fingers. 'It's very beautiful.' The gesture was so unexpected that she shivered and stood up, oddly disturbed by the intimacy of the moment. He rose to his feet. 'Mary painted, too. Did you know?' he said abruptly.

She shook her head. 'I only met her once. Years ago. I'm surprised she remembered me.' But that was a lie. Her own memory was so vivid. Too vivid.

'Would you like to see her work?'

She realised that he was trying to be pleasant. 'Yes, thank you, I would. If you have time.'

He led the way back downstairs to the study. In the bureau was a large folder. He placed it on the desk and opened it. It was a collection of drawings and water-colours, pictures of Ashbrooke and its surroundings. Holly turned them over. Mary Graham had been an artist of considerable talent.

Joshua looked over her shoulder and removed one of the pictures. For a moment he examined it. 'I hadn't realised how talented she was. She never showed her work.' He raised his eyes to meet hers. 'It must run in the family.' He straightened. 'She has one of your pictures. Did you know?' Holly shook her head and he extended his hand to her. 'Come along. I'll show you.'

The gesture caught her by surprise and without even thinking she laid her fingers on his and allowed him to lead her into the dining-room.

A long water-colour of the Thames at Marlow hung over the sideboard and Holly gasped with pleasure. She had been so pleased with it, so thrilled when the local gallery had agreed to take it. When they had put it in their window she had walked by the shop front at least three times a day in order to see it displayed there and had been almost disappointed when it had sold so quickly. It was as if she had lost something that belonged to her, a feeling that the cheque from her first important sale hadn't quite assuaged. It had always been the same when she sold a picture that she really liked.

'How kind of her to buy it.'

'I've seen it before, of course, but I hadn't realised it was yours until I came in here for a bottle of sherry this afternoon. It's very good.'

Holly half turned to him and realised with something of a shock that he still had her fingers caught between his own. She quickly withdrew them.

'Thank you.'

He let his hand drop to his side. 'It occurs to me that you might wish to go home tomorrow,' he said stiffly. 'Perhaps we should clear up one or two things first. The house, for instance. Do you want me to ask Mrs Austin to look after it for the time being?'

'Until I decide what to do with it that would probably be best.'

She could see that Joshua Kent was making an enormous effort to be polite. Why it should be such a strain was a mystery, but she suddenly knew that she had to get to the bottom of it, clear the air between them once and for all, and she was beginning to suspect the reason.

'How old was Mary?' she asked.

He seemed surprised by her question. 'It's difficult to say. She had that fine, fragile sort of beauty that never seems to age. But I suppose she was in her early forties. Why?'

'You must have loved her very much.'

'Loved her?' For a moment he seemed to consider the question quite seriously and then his face darkened as he realised exactly what she meant. 'So, that's what's going through your head. You think that I was her lover and expected to receive my just deserts in her will?'

Stated baldly it sounded quite horrible and she wished the words had never left her mouth, but they could never be recalled and she pressed on, needing to get to the truth. 'What else can I think? You've made your resentment quite plain enough. Does it sound so implausible?'

For a moment he glared at her, then, to her astonishment, he quite suddenly laughed. He caught her expression and shook his head. 'Frankly, yes.'

Holly felt the slow flood of colour rising to her cheeks. 'Oh, lord, I'm sorry. I didn't think. You're surely married — '

'No, Holly, I'm not married. And I suppose if I'm honest it isn't quite that ridiculous. She was a very beautiful woman and I was certainly very fond of her. But I'm afraid you have the wrong generation of Kents. It was my father who carried something of a torch for Mary.'

'Oh!'

His amusement at her total misreading of the situation seemed to have eased the tension. 'Don't look so tragic, Holly. I'm beginning to understand why.' He offered his hand once more. 'Come on. I don't know about you, but I'm hungry.'

It was late when they settled at a corner table at a small restaurant down on the quay and there were few other diners. While they were waiting for their food Joshua sat back and regarded her thoughtfully.

'I was unbelievably rude to you today.'

'Today?' Holly repeated in mock-astonishment. 'You've been unbelievably rude to me since the moment I first opened my front door to you.'

For a moment she thought he was going to deny it. But he simply shrugged. 'Yes, I suppose I have. And I've no right to judge you when Mary didn't.'

'Judge?' Holly lifted her shoulders, uncomfortable with the word. 'I don't think either of us has anything to congratulate ourselves for. The truth of the matter is that the very mention of a funeral upsets me.'

'You're rather young to have much experience of them,' he said.

'Old enough. I was just twelve when Dad died. He had a heart attack somewhere abroad and his body had to be flown home. I didn't really understand what had happened and it all rather frightened me. Then my mother was hit by a car a couple of years ago.' She looked up. 'It wasn't the driver's fault. She just stepped out, not looking. Her head must have been full of

Christmas. She always loved it, couldn't wait to put the tree up. We always did that together on Christmas Eve and then had a little party, just the two of us, for my birthday. I haven't put up decorations since.'

'I'm sorry. I hadn't realised quite what an ordeal it must have been for you today.'

Holly toyed with her fork. 'I was dreading it,' she admitted. 'But it was different, somehow. Not depressing. Who were all those people?'

'Friends, mostly. Some were people Mary had helped. She founded a charity to provide holidays for children. That's how I got to know her so well. She dragged me in to help with fund-raising and when she set her heart on something you didn't stand a chance.'

'Is that why you're her executor?'

'More or less. My father was a solicitor here in Ashbrooke and he was originally named as her executor. When he retired she said she ought to have someone who was likely to outlive her.' His face softened. 'Very brave. She must have known, even then.'

'I wish I'd known her.'

'Do you, Holly?' He leaned forward. 'Then why on earth didn't you come — ?'

The arrival of their supper interrupted the question and, in the business of serving food and wine, it was lost. Or maybe he just decided it was not important enough to pursue. But she decided it was. 'I didn't come, Joshua, because I didn't know she was ill. If you'd let me know before . . . it was too late . . . '

'It was her decision, Holly. She gave me that folder for you — she wanted you to know that she had always cared about what happened to you, despite everything. She didn't blame you for not wanting to know her.' He drew back. 'But you were the loser.'

'But that's not true.' Or was it? Once, writing Christmas cards, she had been on the point of asking her mother if they should send one to Mary. Something had stopped her. 'I hadn't seen her since I was seven years old,' she said defensively.

'She thought it best. She didn't tell me, but clearly something happened then that made her decide it was better to stay away.'

Holly felt a chill along her spine. She didn't need Joshua Kent to tell her what had happened. 'But she told you everything else?'

'She needed to confide in someone.' He stirred the food around his plate with a fork. 'I think she thought someone younger wouldn't be so shocked when she told them that she had an illegitimate daughter.'

'Daughter?' Holly sat for a moment while the words sank in. Then quite suddenly everything was clear. All that talk about her conscience, his grim disapproval. She could hardly blame him, she thought as she raised her hand to her temple, feeling faint. Shock always had that effect on her. She needed air.

Joshua swore softly under his breath, at her side in a heartbeat, his arm around her. 'You didn't know.' It wasn't a question and she didn't bother to confirm or deny it.

'Will you take me back to the hotel?' she asked, struggling to her feet.

'Holly?'

'Now, please. Straight away.'

His brow creased in concern. 'Yes, of course.' He signalled to the waiter and signed the bill. He paused before starting the car, as if he would say something, but the deathly pale set of her face stopped him.

He drew up outside the hotel and she fumbled with the door, wanting to get away from him as quickly as she could. But her brain didn't seem to be sending the right messages to her fingers. He reached across and took her hands and held them in his own, turning her towards him. 'Holly, I'm sorry. Mary thought you knew.'

She glanced down at his hand. It was as if the strength in those long fingers was pouring into her, helping her. Her face when she turned to him was still pale, but her chin was firm, her eyes steady, if a little over-bright.

'There's absolutely no need to apologise. I should have realised right at the beginning that all this was some sort of mistake.'

'Mistake?'

'I'm afraid there's no doubt about it. If you came to my house looking for Mary Graham's illegitimate daughter, you were misled, Mr Kent. You've found the wrong girl.'

'Wrong girl?' His face was all shadows, unreadable. 'What are you talking about? Of course I haven't found the wrong girl. I was looking for Holly Carpenter. I found her.' He shook her slightly as if this would make her see sense. 'I found you.'

'But I am not Mary's daughter.'

'Holly, please. I can see you're upset. It must have been a shock. But it really doesn't matter.'

She turned on him. 'How could you

possibly know that? If your opinion of your own infallibility is so great that it hurts to admit you are wrong, then I'm sorry. But on this occasion you will simply have to accept that you are.'

Stronger now in her anger, she moved to go, but his hand tightened, detaining her. 'There's no possibility of a mistake.'

'On the contrary, Joshua. I'm Holly Carpenter. My mother was Margaret Carpenter and my father was Peter Carpenter. That's the truth and the end of it.'

'And the folder? Why the hell do you think she garnered every scrap of information she could about you? It was more than simple curiosity, wouldn't you say?' His grey eyes glittered angrily, convinced as he was that she was simply refusing to accept a self-evident truth.

'I don't know.' But that wouldn't do. He would have to be convinced that he was wrong. She shook her head from side to side, trying to wipe out the memory of that small bundle of paper that represented her life. 'Perhaps she took a special interest in her cousin's child, a child about the same age as her own daughter?' There was no softening in that cold face. 'If what you say is true, that would be understandable,' she offered, unaware of the pleading note in her voice.

But he was relentless. 'You are her daughter, Holly. She told me your name and where to find you. God knows, I wanted to come and fetch you before . . . but she wouldn't let me. It had been your decision, she said, and she accepted that. She just wanted, hoped that you would finally relent and come to her funeral.'

'If I had known she was ill I would have been happy to come and see her, but no one told me. And I'm not her daughter.'

His mouth was drawn in a hard line. 'Damn you, Holly; I know you're wrong. I know you're Mary's daughter and somehow I'll prove it to you.'

'I'm sorry. That is just not possible.'

She finally pulled free of his grasp. 'Goodnight, Joshua.'

She moved too quickly for him to open the door for her, but he was at her side as she entered the hotel. 'Will you be all right?' he asked.

'Yes, of course,' she said. 'There's no need to see me to my room.'

He ignored this, turning her towards the stairs. 'It's been a trying day, Holly. Sleep on it,' he urged as he opened her door. 'We'll talk again tomorrow. We'll sort something out.'

'Talking won't help, Joshua,' she said.

'Hiding from the truth won't help, either,' he said, losing patience in the face of her intransigence. 'But it's clearly something you've picked up from Margaret Carpenter. I'll see you in the morning.' He turned and walked quickly away.

She closed the door and for a while leaned against it, desperately trying to sort out her confused thoughts. Nothing made sense. She wasn't adopted, she knew that. But one thing was certain — she wasn't planning to stay in Ashbrooke to be hectored by Joshua Kent. It was too late to leave immediately. She would have to spend another night at Ashbrooke Hall, but she made enquiries about the train service and booked a taxi for seven-thirty the following morning. Then she packed her bag, leaving her trousers and sweater ready for the morning.

Not that she slept. She felt stifled by the heavy drapery around the four-poster and disturbed by her own unhappy thoughts. When finally she drifted off in the early hours, she dreamed that she was searching desperately for something, but didn't know what.

A tap on the door finally woke her, releasing her from this misery.

'Come in.'

It was dark in the room, the heavy curtains blocking the early-morning light, but she heard a tray being placed on the table near the bed.

'Thank you,' she said.

'You asked to be called at six-thirty,

Holly. But I've cancelled your taxi. If you want to go home today, I'll take you.'

She struggled up from the depths of the great bed. 'Joshua? What are you doing here?'

He switched on the lamp and sat on the edge of the bed. His hair shone damply in the light, fresh from the shower, and he was dressed casually in jeans that clung to his long legs and a dark polo shirt. 'I was going to have breakfast with Luigi in the kitchen, but I spotted your tray so I volunteered to bring it up to you.' He poured two cups of coffee. 'The croissants are fresh from the oven.'

'I didn't ask for breakfast.'

'No. But since I've missed mine . . . '

'Then you'd better help yourself,' she said, pulling the covers higher as his gaze lingered on her naked shoulders. Having been too hot during the night, she had a dim recollection of throwing off her nightdress. She surreptitiously felt under the bedclothes in the hope of finding it.

Joshua offered her a cup and smiled. 'Your nightdress is on the floor.'

She blushed. 'I was hot in the night,' she said, taking the cup with one hand and hanging on to the sheet with the other. 'These drapes . . . '

'I know,' he said sympathetically. 'But then, I never wear anything in bed to start with. It's so much simpler.'

She swallowed. 'Would you pass it to me?'

He bent and picked up the long plain black satin nightdress, dangling it from his fingers by the shoe-string straps. 'Pretty.'

'Please, Joshua.' He offered it to her, then watched with amusement as she tried to juggle the cup and the sheet to take it from him. 'Oh, go away!' she said furiously, giving up.

He laughed softly, but took pity on her and stood up. 'I'll go if you promise that you'll meet me in the main hall at eight.'

His words were a stark reminder of the real reason for this early call. 'And if

I don't?' she asked.

His mouth curved in a provoking little smile as he twitched the night-gown out of her reach. 'I'll just have to stay here and make sure you do.'

'I promise,' she said quickly. Anything to get rid of him.

'What a pity.' He let the nightgown trickle through his fingers on to the bed, where it made a dark patch against the coverlet.

The minute he was through the door she flew to it and locked it, then went to shower. She was ready long before eight o'clock, but it was exactly on the hour that she walked down the stairs and into the reception area.

Joshua was waiting and took her bag. 'There's no need to do this, you know,' she said. 'If you take me into Exeter I can quite easily catch a train.'

He opened the car door, ignoring this one last attempt to escape from him, and she climbed in without further protest.

'I've been looking through Mary's

papers,' he said as he headed the car towards the motorway.

'And did you find anything?' She found herself almost holding her breath, but that was silly. There was nothing to find.

He shook his head. 'No, Holly. Not a thing. The folder contained everything that referred to you.'

'So why didn't you just let me leave?'

'A number of reasons. If I'm right . . . '

'You are not right! Why do you have to be so damned obstinate?'

He threw her an exasperated glance. 'And you're not being stubborn, I suppose?' She didn't answer. Satisfied that he had made his point, he went on. 'If I'm right there must be papers somewhere. Your house is the obvious place to look.'

'There are no papers.'

They paused at a junction and he turned to her and fixed her with a look that pinned her back in her seat. 'When I came to see you, Holly, I was angry. I had spent the previous week watching a friend die and as far as I was concerned you were an uncaring, thoughtless girl who had taken a quite calculating decision to cut her mother out of her life. I didn't want to like you.'

'You made that plain enough.'

'Your first reaction to my news only reinforced those feelings. The rejection seemed so utterly callous.'

'I didn't mean — '

'No. I realise that. But Mary thought you knew the truth; your mother — Margaret Carpenter — had promised to tell you — '

'There was nothing to tell, Joshua. Why won't you simply accept that?'

'Because of this.' He slipped an envelope from the breast-pocket of his shirt and handed it to her.

She didn't want to take the envelope, but she knew that he wouldn't let this go until she had done as he asked.

'What is it?' she asked as they moved on.

'It's a photograph. I want you to look at it.'

Her fingers trembled as she pulled at the flap and tipped the photograph on to her lap. Then she frowned. It was a photograph of her . . . no, not her, someone very like her. Someone with the same almond-shaped eyes, but blue, not light brown, the same wide, high cheekbones, the full mouth. Holly unconsciously touched her hair. Silver-blonde hair that hung in a smooth curve to her shoulder. She turned the photograph over and there was the stamp of a photographer in Ashbrooke and the date, fifteen years earlier.

'Who is this?' she demanded. But she didn't need an answer. She remembered the look on his face when she had pulled off her hat and he had seen her hair for the first time. 'It's Mary, isn't it?'

'Is it, Holly? It could be you.'

Why hadn't she realised how alike they were? Except that she had only been seven and they hadn't been alike then. She had been a rather thin and scrawny child, not at all like the woman in the photograph.

'You do see now, Holly? You can see why I know I'm right.'

'No! It's just a family likeness. Coincidence.' His expression was compelling her to some unacceptable truth and somehow she had to make him see, prove to him that he was wrong. 'I have my birth certificate,' she said. 'It's at home; I'll show you. As soon as we get there. I'll show you.' Her voice broke on a sob as she turned to him. 'You'll see then, Joshua. You'll have to believe me then.'

4

Joshua wanted to stop, give Holly a chance to recover her composure, but she refused. 'I want to get home as quickly as possible,' she said, unmovable in her determination, and after the briefest glance at her set face he had humoured her, putting his foot down when they reached the motorway and keeping it there, his concentration focused only on the road.

It was lunchtime when he finally pulled up outside her home and the two of them sat for a moment, adjusting themselves to the stillness. Then Holly roused herself. 'Thank you, Joshua.'

'What for?'

'Understanding that I didn't want to talk.'

He shrugged. 'I'll get your bag.'

She put her hand on his arm, detaining him. 'That will wait. I'll get that birth certificate and then I'll make you some lunch.'

He watched as she searched through the sideboard drawer. 'I had it recently,' she said desperately, when her shaking fingers couldn't find it. 'I had to get a new passport from the Post Office. It must be here. I know it is . . . ' She jumped as he placed a hand on her shoulder and leaned over her. She turned to glance up at him, surprised by the intimacy suggested by the warmth of his body against hers, the simple touch of his hand.

'I believe this is it.' He plucked the document from the drawer and offered it to her.

She forced her mind back to the business in hand. 'Yes, it is. I wonder why I couldn't see it?'

'Maybe you didn't really want to find it?' he suggested.

She made no comment, but took the document from him and spread it on the sideboard, holding it flat. 'Now, there,' she said. 'Will you believe me now?' His breath was sucked in sharply as he read the words the registrar had written in a neat, copperplate hand.

'It's not what I expected.'

'What did you expect?' she demanded. 'An adoption certificate?'

'Frankly, yes. I'm sorry for doubting you, Holly. I knew you wanted to believe it, but I thought you were fooling yourself.' He took the certificate and held it up to the light, checking to see if there had been any illicit alterations. 'But I still don't understand.' He turned to her. 'I'll have to check the original entry, of course, but I have no doubt that this is genuine enough. There has to be another explanation.'

'Well, thank you,' she said with uncharacteristic bitterness, shaken, bewildered by his insistence, in the face of this evidence, that he was right.

'Holly, please try to understand.' His voice was so unexpectedly gentle that her insides flipped over. She moved quickly away and sat down, wrapping her arms around herself.

'No, Joshua,' she begged. 'Just go away and forget you ever came here.'

But there was no escape. He came and squatted on his heels in front of her. 'I was told by a dying woman that you were her daughter.' He pushed back a dark strand of hair that had fallen over his forehead. 'It was hard enough to believe that she had a child. For her to admit that she had given it . . . you, Holly . . . given you away to be brought up by someone else was an agony for her. If you had known her you would understand.'

'I'll never understand why you're putting me through this,' she said, rising quickly, needing to move, not wanting to hear him, and he let her go, straightening behind her, but said nothing. 'Are you sure she wasn't . . . ?' Holly hesitated, turning to him. 'She must have been on some sort of drugs for the pain — '

'You think she was imagining all this?'

'Isn't it possible?' Her voice pleaded with him.

'No.' He dismissed the idea without hesitation. 'Are there any other family papers?'

Her shoulders sagged. He wasn't going to give up unless she convinced him, but she didn't know how. 'A few. Marriage certificates, death certificates. That sort of thing. They're upstairs, but they won't tell you anything.'

'Nothing else? Letters, diaries? What about the loft?'

'I don't know. There are a few boxes stored up there, but nothing important. I haven't been up there in ages — '

'Perhaps we should — '

The key in the door stopped him and he turned as David appeared in the doorway and, eyes narrowed, glanced from Holly to Joshua and back again.

'How's the heiress, then?' he said, casually dropping a kiss on her cheek before she could anticipate the gesture and avoid it. 'Are we celebrating tonight?'

'No — '

But Joshua forestalled her, his voice

wintry as he took in the casual way David had draped his arm around her shoulders. 'I'm afraid you'll have to wait to celebrate Holly's legacy. There has been a slight hitch.'

'Oh?' David said sharply. 'What sort of hitch?' he asked suspiciously.

'It's nothing much,' she said quickly, in case Joshua might take it in his head to explain. But Joshua made no such mistake. There was an awkward silence and, to fill it, she quickly introduced the two men.

'Joshua, this is David Grantham. I share the house with him,' she added, because she hated the word lodger, but clearly some explanation was necessary. 'David, Joshua Kent, my cousin's executor.'

'Joshua Kent?' David was suddenly all smiles and offered his hand. It was taken briefly. 'I thought you looked familiar. This is a great pleasure. I've heard a great deal about you. Can I offer you a drink?'

'I'm just about to make some lunch for Mr Kent, David,' Holly said quickly, hoping to head him off.

'Great. We can have a chat over one of Holly's omelettes. She's a great cook.'

Joshua ignored this and when he turned to Holly his face had returned to the aloof, unreadable expression of the man who had called two days earlier. 'I can't stay for lunch, Holly,' he said. 'I'll get your bags from the car.'

She followed him out. 'I'm sorry, Joshua. David's — '

'You don't have to explain,' he said curtly, opening the boot. He extracted her bag. 'But we still have to examine the papers in the loft.'

'Not now.' She would have enough trouble damping David's curiosity as it was. He was ambitious enough to realise the potential in this sort of human-interest story. Friendship would count for nothing if there was a chance of breaking into the nationals.

'Tomorrow, then.' And she knew there was no point in arguing.

'If you must, but I have to work in the morning. Come after two o'clock.

You can search the house if you want, so long as you promise that if you don't find anything you'll stop all this nonsense.'

'And if we do find something?' he persisted, placing her bag in the hall.

'We won't.' She shook her head at the sharp question in his eyes. 'I shan't go up to the loft before you and destroy the evidence, Joshua. You'll be the first person up there in several years. I offer the dust as my alibi.' She managed a smile. After all, she had been right and could afford to be generous. 'I have a particular aversion to spiders.'

He reached out and touched the platinum curve of her hair. 'Something else you have in common with Mary. Until tomorrow, then.' It was a while before she moved, then she slowly closed the door and turned back into the living-room.

She picked up the birth certificate and gently smoothed out the folds.

'What's that?' David asked, coming from the kitchen with a beer.

'My birth certificate,' she said, and touched the date. December the twenty-fourth. Christmas Eve. Her mother had said she was the best Christmas present she'd ever had. Now, quite suddenly, the words seemed to take on a different meaning.

★　★　★

'The boyfriend not at home?'

'Who? Oh, David. No, we won't be disturbed today. He's at the magistrates' court all afternoon.'

'Really? A parking ticket, or can I hope it's something more serious?'

'Neither,' she said, surprised into giggling. 'He works for the local paper.'

'Far more serious, then,' he said with a barb to his voice. 'We'd better get on with the search party, before he comes back and scents a story.'

Joshua had come prepared for a foray into the loft dressed in a pair of old jeans and a sweatshirt. He looked so much younger out of a suit that her suggestion that he was Mary's lover seemed embarrassing in retrospect. He must have women falling over themselves. Young, beautiful women. She remembered the look that Lisa Stamford had given him and wondered if they were lovers. The sharp stab of jealousy was so unexpected that she almost gasped. 'The ladder is in the shed,' she said quickly.

'Lead the way,' he said and she did, thankful that he was totally unaware of the impossible thoughts racketing around her head. But his strong, reassuring arm at her back was oddly disturbing.

A few minutes later the ladder was propped against the loft-hatch and the trouble he had opening it dispelled any doubts he might harbour that she had been there ahead of him.

She steadied it while he pushed at it with the heel of his hand, unable to take her eyes from the firm, well-muscled line of his thighs as he strained upwards. It finally shifted with a small shower of dust and she turned away with an exclamation as it covered her.

'All right?' He glanced down at her. 'No spiders?'

She shuddered involuntarily. 'Don't!'

He laughed and disappeared into the darkness. She could see the swing of the torch he had brought with him as he crawled across the joists.

'You could do with some insulation up here,' his voice came hollowly back to her.

'Tell me something I don't know,' she called back.

His head appeared in the hatchway, a provoking grin doing disturbing things to his mouth. 'Where shall I begin?'

Her voice caught in her throat. Perhaps it was the dust. 'Just get on with it,' she urged him hoarsely.

He hung there for a moment, very still. 'From anyone else, Holly Carpenter, I'd take that as an invitation.' He didn't wait to see her sudden blush, but disappeared into the darkness and for a while she heard him moving about above her. When he finally reappeared he handed a dust-covered box down to her. 'This is the only possibility. It's not heavy.'

Holly took the box. He was right, it wasn't heavy, but it was sealed up with tape and had clearly not been disturbed for a long time. She had no recollection of seeing it on her admittedly infrequent trips into the roof space.

He joined her on the landing, and she dragged her eyes back from the box to him.

'Have you any idea what's in here?' he asked.

She shook her head. 'I've never seen this before.'

'It was right at the back,' he said. 'I don't believe it was meant to be found by any but the most persistent searcher.'

'And you are certainly that,' she said unhappily. She had been so sure. But now, looking at this battered box that had once held nothing more interesting than typing paper, she knew, deep inside, that there was something to be discovered. And all she was certain of now was that she didn't want to know what it was.

'I have no choice, Holly. You must see that.'

'Haven't you? Couldn't you just put this back and pretend you never saw it?'

He took the box from her. 'You know I can't. If you are right I will have to start looking for someone else.'

'But you don't think I'm right.'

'Mary would never have been that careless.'

'Wouldn't she? You're quite prepared to believe she was careless enough to give away her child.'

His mouth hardened. 'There's no point in standing here arguing about it.' He turned away and went quickly down the stairs. She followed him a good deal more slowly and when she reached the living-room the box was already on the table and he had opened a pocket knife in order to slit the tape.

'Wait!'

He straightened and after one glance at her white face he handed her the knife. She pushed in the point, but her look was pleading as she hesitated, hoping even now that he would change his mind.

'It's like pulling off a sticking-plaster, Holly,' he urged her. 'The quicker you do it, the less painful it is in the end.'

'Is that a guarantee?'

'Life doesn't come with guarantees.'

'No, I suppose not.' She took a firmer grip on the knife and sliced quickly through the tape, then let the knife fall with a clatter to the floor as she dropped to her knees and pulled at the lid. Inside was a thick, padded enve-lope. There was nothing written on it but her name. It must have been bought especially for this purpose.

Joshua lifted it out and held it for a moment before handing it to her.

She smoothed over the envelope, turned it over. Read her name again.

'Do you want to be on your own while you open it, Holly?' Joshua asked.

She shook her head. 'No. You'd better stay and see it through.' The truth of the matter was she needed him with her. Needed his strength. She opened the envelope and tipped its contents on to the table.

Until then she had still hoped that it wasn't true. That her birth certificate wasn't a lie. That her mother hadn't given her away. There wasn't much to tell her that her hope was groundless. A man's linen handkerchief, half a theatre ticket, a bunch of pressed violets pinned to a card, their colour as fresh as the day they were picked, a tiny gold locket and a thick notebook. Five small items. She sat back on her heels, stuffing her fist into her mouth to prevent the cry of dismay.

The air was so still, so fragile that she knew that if she moved, if she touched them, her whole life, everything she had trusted, known, would disappear for ever.

But it already had. This hidden cache was proof that there was some great secret and that nothing would ever be the same again.

She picked up each item in turn. The violets, the handkerchief, which had somehow absorbed their lingering scent, the theatre ticket, torn in half by some unknown hand twenty-five years before. The locket sprang open to her touch to reveal a small curl of light brown hair. Not her hair or Mary's. It belonged to a man who had fathered her and then simply abandoned them both without a thought. Finally, the notebook, covered in Chinese brocade, with its own gold pen. A precious thing.

She swallowed and ran the tip of her tongue nervously over her lips before looking up to meet the grave expression on Joshua Kent's face.

'Like sticking-plaster?' she asked shakily.

'Would you prefer me to read it?' he asked.

She shook her head. It had been waiting for her and after a last, brief hesitation she found the courage to open the book, written years before and left, like a time bomb, for her to find.

The handwriting was beautiful. Mary had written her thoughts and feelings from the first moment she had fallen in love. They were rare, bright, new and needed all the care she could give them.

It took Holly a long time to read and in all that time the man beside her said not a word. There were so many words. So much joy and so much pain and towards the end the pages had been blotted with tears.

It was only when she reached the postscript, written years after, that finally a great choking sob escaped her and she dropped the book, unable to read through the film of tears. Joshua caught her and drew her close, holding her against him, letting her pour her grief on to his broad chest.

She was barely aware of his soothing words, only that he stroked her hair, enfolding her in his strength, only that here was comfort. His cheek was cool against her temple; his lips brushed the delicate skin there and she raised her tear-soaked eyes to his. 'Holly,' he murmured. 'I'm so sorry.' For a moment he seemed to hesitate, then, briefly, for the endless space of a heartbeat, his lips touched hers and in that magic she was able to forget everything else. Smiling a little, he brushed the hair back from her face with his fingers and produced a handkerchief to dry her eyes. When he had finished, he asked, 'Have you got any brandy?'

She shook her head. 'Unless there's some left over from Christmas.'

He found a bottle and poured some of the amber liquid into a glass which he pressed into her hands. 'Drink this.' She pulled a face. She had never much liked brandy. 'Purely medicinal,' he said firmly.

'Medicinal?'

'It'll make you feel better.' She looked at it doubtfully, but she drank it in one swallow and shuddered and coughed as it burned its way down her throat.

He slapped her on the back until she had recovered. 'I meant you to sip it,' he scolded, but gently.

'I don't like the taste.' She saw his eyes stray towards the notebook, lying where it had fallen, on the floor. 'No. Please don't read it.'

'I need to know, Holly.'

She closed her eyes. 'You were right. Mary was my mother.'

'The birth certificate?'

'It wasn't a deliberate deceit. It just happened. She used my mother's — ' She stopped and carefully corrected herself. 'She used Margaret Carpenter's name at the clinic. They always notify the local health authority of births, apparently, and as I was on the records as Holly Carpenter there didn't seem any point in owning up and putting it right. Apparently, Margaret and Peter were going to adopt me anyway. This saved them the bother.'

He frowned at the sharp bitterness in her voice.

'I spent a lot of time thinking about it last night. That Mary had used your mother's name seemed the only possibility.'

'She wasn't my mother,' Holly said. 'Neither of them was.'

'That's not true.'

'Isn't it?' She turned on him. 'One of them didn't have me, one of them didn't want me.'

He grasped her shoulders and held her at arm's length. 'Nothing's ever that simple, Holly. When you've had time to think about it, I'm certain you'll see it differently.'

'I doubt it.' She picked up one of the pathetic remnants of the brief affair. 'This belonged to my father.' She held out the handkerchief. 'How would you feel if that was all you knew of your father?'

He saw the hurt, tried to help. 'Perhaps I could find out more for you. It shouldn't be impossible. Even after all this time.'

'No! He thought too much of his position in society to risk it for Mary, to acknowledge my existence. I don't want to know anything about him.'

'Not now. But perhaps one day . . . '

He shrugged. 'It's too easy for me to tell you not to judge them. I have no way of knowing what you're feeling. Or what they felt at the time.'

'Not enough apparently.' She hated herself. Her father might not have wanted her, but Mary . . . It hurt. The pain was so deep that she thought she could die of it. 'They should have told me.'

'Yes. They should have told you. But Mary thought you knew. Margaret had promised her that you would be told when you came of age. And presumably that she'd give you this.' He indicated the contents of the box.

'But she didn't.'

'Perhaps Margaret Carpenter still thought of twenty-one as that special birthday. Or maybe it was just easier to put it off for as long as possible. She died a few days before your birthday, didn't she, Holly?'

'Yes,' she said, choking back a cry as the reason for her abstraction struck home. She began to push the memories of old desires back into their envelope in an effort to consign them to the past where they belonged.

Joshua reached out and caught her wrist, stopping her. 'What do you intend to do?'

'Do?'

'Come back to Ashbrooke with me,' he said, drawing her into his arms, but she resisted this new attempt to comfort her. It would be too easy to be comforted by Joshua Kent. He knew all the right words. But then he would go away, back to Lisa Stamford or some other woman like her, and there would be no comfort in the world to make that hurt better.

'Ashbrooke?' she asked, then shook her head decisively. 'It's too late for that.'

'Not necessarily. There's the house.'

She refused to meet his eye. 'Do what you like with it, Joshua. I don't want it.'

'Think about it for a while,' he pressed her.

'No. I never want to go there again.'

She deliberately made her voice hard.

'If you're sure. But you'll have to decide — '

'You decide, Joshua,' she said wearily. 'I have to go to work.'

He frowned. 'I thought you worked this morning.'

'Just catching up with paperwork before the end of term. I have a class this evening. My last one.'

'Oh, yes. You'll want to say goodbye to everyone.'

'Goodbye?'

'Surely you'll resign now? You won't carry on teaching?'

'Resign? Why should I do that, Joshua?' she asked with biting irony. 'Because my mother — not the one who brought me up, but the new one I didn't know about, the one who gave me away — has left me all her money as a sop to her guilt?'

His head shot back as if she had hit him and he let her wrist drop. The breaking of the link between them and his step back, putting a clear space between them, left her quite alone, as if she had somehow been cast adrift.

'Very well, I'll get on with it,' he said impassively. 'I've already had an excellent offer for Highfield — Mary's house.' He waited, his face without emotion, for some reaction. There was none. 'Do you need any money straight away?'

'No,' she said. Then she lifted her chin defiantly. 'Wait. Yes, I do need some.' He raised a brow in query. 'I'm going to Italy at the weekend.'

'How much do you want?'

The question disconcerted her. She had expected him to be angry with her. Had intended him to be angry.

'I don't know.'

'I'll transfer five thousand pounds; that should cover every possibility. Give me the details of your bank account and I'll see to it first thing in the morning.'

★ ★ ★

'Falling asleep in the sun is not wise, Holly.'

The voice came from far away, familiar and yet strange after the weeks in Italy and France. An English voice that sent a ripple of pleasure up her spine. She kept her eyes closed, afraid that she had imagined it. But a shadow moved across her face and blocked out the sun.

'I'm not asleep,' she murmured.

'I know.' The voice was teasing. 'You're simply resting your eyes.'

If she had allowed herself to wonder what Joshua's reaction might be to her continued absence, she would have decided that he wouldn't much care. She certainly wouldn't have expected him to come looking for her, not after their last meeting.

He had arrived unexpectedly on her doorstep the day after they had found the box in the loft, to confirm the details of transfer of money to her account. She had opened the door and he had been there, grave, courteous, keeping his distance in the face of her brittle temper. It was the only time in her life she had wished she had been on the telephone. Then he would simply have called her and she wouldn't have had to bear the watchful scrutiny in his eyes.

He had asked carefully if she was all right, if she had slept and, on her snappy assurance that she was just fine, he had resisted any further enquiries, and had simply told her that he would call again and see her when she returned from Italy.

'I'd like a little notice, Joshua. I may not be in if you just turn up,' she warned him.

He'd looked at her hard and she'd thought he was about to say something, but he'd clearly thought better of it, since he'd contented himself with a slight shrug and said, 'You could come up to the office if you prefer. I'll drop you a line when everything is settled and you can call me and arrange a time.'

But she hadn't been there to call

him. She'd taken her flight to Florence the next day and, when the three weeks had expired, simply not gone home.

She lifted lids so heavy that the effort was almost insupportable, unwilling to face the man who had come to disturb her fragile peace, half expecting him to be dressed in one of those elegant suits, tailored to perfection for his broad shoulders. But he looked equally at home in a fine jersey shirt and tailored shorts, his bare feet pushed into a pair of espadrilles. In fact, she thought, it was almost shocking that one man could look quite so desirable.

And desire was the right word. Because, although Margaret and Mary had been in her thoughts during the past weeks, Joshua had been there too. Not the angry, disapproving man to whom she had opened her door that disastrous afternoon, but a different man entirely — the one who had put his arms around her, holding her close while she had cried her heart out. A man who had kissed her because her heart was breaking. Maybe all that was tied up in her unwillingness to return. A quite ridiculous complication. He had merely been kind, although *kind* was not a word she associated with Joshua Kent. And she doubted that he could ever be described as *merely* anything.

'I've brought some lunch,' he said, putting down a wicker basket, as if this were sufficient explanation for his sudden appearance, and folded himself up beside her on the hard, dry earth.

Holly forced her eyes up from the pleasurable contemplation of his square shoulders, the strong, tanned column of his neck, to the more dangerous territory of his face, and suddenly she was wide awake.

'How did you find me?' she asked.

'I saw your car parked on the road. They told me what you were driving at the hotel.'

She made an impatient, dismissive gesture. 'I didn't mean that. How did you know where to look in the first place?'

'Were you hiding?' One dark brow flicked up in apparent amusement at her naïveté. He began to open a bottle of wine dewed with moisture. 'You'll have to try a little harder if you're being serious about it.'

'Of course I wasn't hiding, but . . . '

'But?' he asked, an edge to his voice warning her that he expected an answer.

'But nothing,' she said. 'I just didn't go out of my way to let anyone know where I was. That's all.'

'No, but you sent David a postcard from Arles. You hired a car and bought some clothes using a credit card. Finding someone is not so difficult if you know the right computer to ask.'

'And I'm sure *you* know them all personally.'

'A few,' he conceded, apparently not at all put out by the irritation in her voice. 'Try this.' He handed her a glass of wine and then proceeded to tear hunks of bread off a loaf. 'Cheese? Or there's some pâté,' he offered.

She ignored his offer of food. 'All right, Joshua, you've proved how clever you are. Now perhaps you'd like to tell me exactly why you're here?'

'But you know why I've come, Holly.' He looked up then, his eyes creasing against the fierce sun. 'I've come to take you home.'

5

'Home?' Holly said. Then the realisation of his arrogance hit her like a sledge hammer and she exploded. 'You've got some kind of nerve, Joshua. I'll come home when I'm good and ready.'

He was unmoved by this outburst. 'Your prolonged absence is causing me problems. I need signatures on some documents and decisions have to be made about property.'

'Why? Surely nothing is that urgent?'

'It won't take long,' he said, as if this was sufficient reason for her to comply with his wishes. He scooped a piece of ripe Brie on to a crust. 'You can come back when everything is tidied up. If you want to.'

'Well, thank you, sir,' she said, fury at his casual hijacking of her life striking amber sparks in her wide eyes. 'You are too kind.'

The tiny fan of white lines around his eyes disappeared as he smiled. 'I'm glad you see it that way. For a moment I thought you were going to be difficult.'

'Difficult?' She drew a deep breath, determined to show him exactly how difficult she could be. But then she stopped. Why she couldn't exactly have said. It took a great deal to provoke her to anger but once aroused nothing and no one could stop her until she had given vent to her feelings. Something warned her that it wouldn't make any impression on Joshua Kent. 'When you've gone to so much trouble?' she said, suddenly all sweet compliance.

She was rewarded with a sharp, appraising glance. She had surprised him and that was recompense enough for her restraint. 'It was no trouble,' he said.

'But surely a telephone call would have done?' she persisted. 'Why did you have to come yourself?'

'I thought you might be pleased to see me.' The corner of his mouth tugged upwards in an ironic parody of a smile and she had the grace to blush for her lack of manners. 'And I'm Mary's executor. There is no one else. You'll forgive me if I suggest you would not have simply packed up and come home if I'd telephoned and asked you to? Or even if I had used your preferred method of communication and written a letter.' He waited a moment, then smiled with a sweetness to match her own, just to prove that he, too, could be good when he wanted. Then he quite spoiled the effect by adding, 'Of course, I could be wrong.'

'And when was the last time you were wrong about anything?' The words flew from her mouth, the careful control snapping like an overstretched rubber band.

He thought for a moment. 'Well, in 1970, I bet my father a pound that the England football team would win the World Cup,' he offered.

'1970? As recently as that?' And suddenly she found it necessary to suppress a giggle firmly. 'No, that won't do,' she said, once she had established control over her features. 'You could only have been . . . ' She pushed her hair back and, propping her chin on her knees, considered for a moment, taking full advantage of this opportunity to study his face openly. Here, in the open air and sunshine, he looked so much younger than that first grim impression. But she wasn't sure; she suddenly wished she hadn't started this.

'Eight,' he said, finally putting her out of her difficulty. He leaned back upon an elbow. 'I'm thirty-two. Since you were obviously wondering.'

'Oh.' She hadn't realised her thoughts were quite that transparent. She leaned quickly forward to cut a piece of cheese, letting the long, fair curtain of her hair fall forward to cover her confusion.

'And the reason for the hurry is that the buyers for Highfield are keen to get on with it,' he said, returning to his original subject.

'Buyers?' She felt an odd little tug at

her heart. 'You have buyers for the house?'

'I did tell you,' he said, patiently.

'Did you?' Her forehead creased in concentration. 'I don't remember.'

'No. Well, you were rather distraught at the time so I didn't press it. I had assumed you would be around when I needed to discuss the details. You didn't bother to tell me that you intended to leave the country for an indefinite period.' He shrugged. 'But they are getting impatient to complete and it is a very good offer.'

She bit back an exclamation that she didn't care about the money. She would have gladly forgone her inheritance if she had just known about Mary before it was too late. But it *was* too late and there was nothing she could do about that. Going back would make no difference.

'Surely I don't have to go back to England?' she objected. 'Let me sign your piece of paper right now, then I won't be a nuisance, wasting your valuable time.'

'Did I say you were a nuisance?' His look was disquieting. 'Besides, it's not that simple. You'll have to decide what to do with the contents of the house. There are some very good pieces of furniture and porcelain and if you don't want to keep any of it I'll have to put it to auction.' She could imagine what he was thinking. She'd better take it because it was a lot better than the stuff she had at home.

'Sell it,' she said roughly.

'Better come and look at it first. Since you're coming home anyway.' His tone suggested that argument would be futile. 'Why don't you have some of these olives? They're very good.' She absently took a small green olive and nibbled it and he poured her another glass of wine. 'But don't worry about the house. We'll sort it all out tomorrow. Tell me about your holiday. You look wonderful.' He lifted his hand to her cheek and stroked it very gently with the back of his fingers. 'Like a ripe peach.'

She abruptly reached for her hat to

move from the disturbing, dangerous intimacy of his touch — then wished she hadn't. Then she called herself every kind of fool. But he prompted her to tell him about her travels, apparently unaware of the agitation he had caused and, relieved to be on less difficult ground, she described her visit to Florence and the art galleries there, and her weeks in the Tuscan hills.

'What made you move on to France?' he asked. 'I had the impression you intended to carry on teaching.'

'You were the one who said I should resign.'

He glanced at her with a slightly jaundiced expression. 'You didn't take too kindly to the suggestion, as I recall.'

'No. And to be honest it wasn't my decision. That last evening at college I discovered that one of the classes was being closed because the education budget was overspent. The teacher involved had a wife and two children and a mortgage.'

'So you volunteered to go in his

place?' She didn't answer. She would have done it, even without the legacy. 'And so you've become a full-time artist. Are you enjoying it?' he asked.

'I'm not sure. Too much of a good thing, perhaps.' She had moved on to Provence hoping to find fresh inspiration in the Roman ruins, pine-clad hills and small terracotta villages, but concentration had been difficult. 'I've been planning the trip to Tuscany for ever,' she said quickly, not wanting to think why it had been difficult. 'But I think I crammed too much in, too quickly.'

'A bit like eating too much chocolate at Christmas?' he suggested.

'A surfeit of old masters?' She smiled at the idea. 'Perhaps. Anyway, I wanted to be quiet, to think. Provence is a bonus from Mary. There was always something more urgent to spend the money on before,' she explained.

'Yes, it was bucketing down with rain when I called at your house last week in the vain hope that you might have returned. I'm afraid your guttering is in dire need of replacement.'

She groaned. 'I hoped it would keep until the autumn. I've been saving the money from David's rent to pay for it.'

'He pays you rent? He gave me the impression . . . ' He let the sentence hang, unfinished.

'What impression?' She saw the small movement, scarcely a shrug, that said more than words ever could and swore a silent oath that David would pay for it. 'He gave you the impression that we live together?' She raised long lashes and regarded Joshua Kent coolly. 'I wonder why?'

His impassive expression was oddly unsettling. 'That's not for me to say. Perhaps he sees me as some sort of threat. Maybe he was simply warning me off.' His look was unwavering.

'You could have put his mind at rest,' she prompted, then mocked herself for being so obvious.

This seemed to amuse him. 'Surely you are in a better position to reassure him than I?' he suggested and she felt hot colour rise to her cheeks. 'Perhaps if you'd let him know where you were, and when you'd be back? One postcard is hardly compensation for not bringing him with you.'

'He's not interested in art.'

'That undoubtedly explains the omission. But I would have thought that during the six weeks you've been away you might have found a little time — ' he looked thoughtful, and it suddenly occurred to her that Joshua might be doing a little prompting on his own account ' — if you had wanted to, that is, to let him know where you were.'

'I was too busy,' she answered, guiltily aware that David had never once entered her thoughts. She raised her eyes to his. 'But you didn't know either. That must have been some comfort to him.'

'You'd have thought so.' He offered a bland smile. 'As soon as you get home you'll be able to explain it all to him yourself.'

'There's nothing to explain.' But Holly silently swore that David would be left in no doubt that if he harboured any thoughts of moving along the corridor to her bedroom he would be looking for somewhere else to live. 'So when do we leave?' she asked.

'In the morning. I've booked two seats from Montpellier. You've plenty of time to finish your drawing.'

She looked at the discarded pad, lying where it had fallen. 'I can't get it right.'

'On the contrary, Holly. It's a remarkable likeness of your mother. She must have made quite an impression on you.'

'Mary has been on my mind.' At night she seemed to call to her. Sometimes the feeling was so strong that it caught her unawares even in the daytime.

He leaned back against a tree and half closed his eyes. 'Tell me,' he said. 'Maybe I can help.'

She hesitated and yet who else would

understand better? 'I was so angry,' she offered tentatively. 'When I said neither of them was my mother . . . ' She didn't know how to go on.

There was no hint of disapproval. He remained relaxed against the trunk of an olive tree, his hands laced behind his head. 'It was a perfectly natural reaction, Holly. There's no need to feel guilty.'

'Isn't there?' She sighed. 'Margaret loved me; she didn't deserve that. She was my mother in every sense of the word that matters. But Mary is crying out to me, Joshua . . . ' She went on to tell Joshua how through the pages of her journal Mary told how she had loved a man with a sweet, wild abandon and carried his child for nine long months. Described how her hands had felt the gradual swelling of her belly, felt the child move and grow strong inside her and all the time she had known that she would have to give her up. It hadn't been an easy option. There had been less awkward ways out of such a problem, even then. But Mary Graham had borne her out of love, and out of love had given her the gift of life. Joshua listened to her stumbling over the words.

Finally he said, 'She made her choice, Holly. I told you that she didn't blame you. She had no right to blame you.'

'You would, if you knew.' She sensed a sudden stillness about him. 'You see, it was all my fault.'

His pose, outwardly relaxed as ever, sharpened. 'But you didn't know — '

'Mary came to see me on my seventh birthday.'

He nodded. 'I know.'

'She brought me a doll; did she tell you that?' He shook his head, leaning forward, all attention now. 'It was very special, too expensive for Mum to buy.' Holly wrapped her arms around her knees and rested her head there so as not to see his eyes. 'It was in a big green and gold box and there were layers of tissue paper. Oh, lord, Joshua, I was so thrilled that I just threw my arms around her and hugged her.' The memory was sharp, bright. Clear as the Provençal sun. 'Then I saw Mum's face, saw that she was crying. I didn't understand, but I knew she was unhappy and I pushed Mary away and ran to her. It was in the journal . . . she decided then not to come back.'

He was beside her in one movement, lifting her face to meet his. 'Don't, Holly. Don't torture yourself. It wasn't your fault; they should have told you. They hurt themselves.'

'I helped.'

'No,' he said fiercely. 'You were seven years old. They were two grown women who between them made a difficult situation impossible.' He took her hands and pulled her to her feet. 'Come on. It's getting far too hot to sit out here. You haven't got the colouring for it.' His fingers trailed through her hair. 'I'll bet you were a hit in Italy,' he said a little roughly.

'Don't remind me,' she groaned.

'After the first day I kept it hidden under a scarf.'

'What idiots men can be,' he said. He smiled slightly. 'If I promise not to pinch your bottom, will you let me take you out tonight?' When she didn't immediately answer he added lightly, 'Unless, of course, you have some great hairy Frenchman a slave at your feet?'

She suddenly laughed, teased out of her gloomy mood. 'I'll give him the night off,' she promised.

★ ★ ★

Joshua had taken a room at the small inn where she had been staying for the past couple of weeks. It was clean, comfortable in a basic sort of way, but hardly his sort of place, she would have thought, and yet he seemed perfectly at home when she went out into the courtyard that evening and found him relaxing over a smoky glass of *pastis* with the *patron*.

The two men looked up as she appeared

and she was glad she had taken so much trouble with her appearance. She had chosen to wear for the first time a new dress, grey and white, one of several she had bought in France. Her hair swung loose in a smooth curtain to her shoulders, bare but for the shoelace straps of her dress, in fairest contrast against the light gold of her tan. Joshua was first to his feet, but the *patron* was swift to leap up and dust off his chair and hold it for her, before making his excuses and, with a look of infinite regret, leaving her alone with Joshua.

He sat for a moment and regarded her intently.

'What is it?' she asked, convinced that she must have a smudge on the end of her nose. 'What's wrong?'

He shook his head. 'Nothing. I was just thinking that coming to fetch you was one of my better ideas.'

'Oh,' she said, disconcerted by this declaration. 'I think that was a compliment.'

'You think right. Shall we go?'

'Where are you taking me?'

'On a mystery tour. Will you place yourself entirely in my hands?' He held her with his eyes for a moment, demanding that she trust him, and she felt every nerve-ending stir.

She nodded, once, her face quite pale, and he took her hand, tucking it into the warm crook of his arm. His hired Peugeot was parked in the square and as he opened the door a blast of hot air met them. 'It'll soon cool down, when we're moving,' he promised as she pulled a face.

He headed towards the exciting, marshy delta of the Rhône and once in a while Joshua pointed out something of interest, or some place he had visited and was sure she would like too, asking where she had been and what she had seen.

'I think I've done too much sightseeing. I went to Gordes to see the Vasarély in the chateau last week and vowed that was the last. I'm afraid I enjoyed the boutiques far more.'

'Is that where you bought the dress?' he asked.

'Don't you know, Joshua?' she asked in apparent amazement. 'You'd better check my credit card statement on your friendly computer,' she suggested and was rewarded with an appreciative grin.

The sun quietly died as they drove towards the delta, leaving the evening sky full of pinks and purples that reflected magically on occasional glimpses of flat water and turned a startled herd of wild horses from white to momentary amethyst.

It was dark by the time they drove into the square of a small white-painted town. Joshua edged the car down a narrow lane and then into the courtyard of a house that stood above the dark sea. 'We've arrived,' he said, opening the door for her.

'Yes, but where exactly are we?' she asked. Then she knew. The man that walked across the courtyard to meet them was a reflection of Joshua. Older, paler, the hair had never been so dark and was now well-salted with grey and his son had outgrown him in stature and build. But, despite his nearing sixty, Joshua's father was still a man who would turn heads wherever he went, Holly thought.

'I'm so glad you've come, Holly,' he said, holding out both hands to her. 'Joshua has told me all about you.' And after a moment in which he seemed to drink in the presence of the fair, slender girl, he bent and kissed her cheek.

Then he put his arm around her shoulder and led her to a chair. 'Sit down, my dear. Joshua will get us a drink and then we'll have dinner.'

The evening was spent quite simply. They ate wonderful food, drank a little wine and talked. About France, about art. But whenever Holly looked up she found Mr Kent's eyes fixed upon her. Once she glanced at Joshua, a question in her eyes, but, with the smallest shake of his head, he reassured her. He had not told his father the truth of her birth. He clearly considered that something only she had the right to do. And she wasn't ready to talk about it yet.

'Thank you for coming to see me, Holly. Joshua must bring you again when you're both not in quite so much hurry,' he said as he walked them back to the car. 'Or, if he's too busy to bring you, come yourself and stay, any time. I look forward to getting to know you better.'

She took his hand and he held it briefly for a second before turning away and, in the steady glow of the shuttered candle on the table, she thought she saw his eyes glisten and remembered that Joshua had told her that his father had loved Mary.

They were both silent as Joshua drove swiftly back through the darkness, but when they stopped once more in the village square he turned away from the hotel.

'I thought we might take a walk by the river and have a cognac,' he offered in reply to her questioning glance.

She nodded, but said, 'I'll stick to coffee.' They began to stroll towards a café by the river. 'I liked your father. Thank you for taking me to see him.' Then, because it was somehow important, she asked, 'It was him you came to see, wasn't it? Not me.'

'I spent yesterday with him, Holly. We had some business to sort out. But, unlike you, he's not averse to using the telephone. The only purpose of my journey was to take you home.' His expression was unreadable in the shadowy light, but his voice was utterly convincing.

'Why?'

He seemed oddly disconcerted by her directness. 'You were running away, Holly. Don't make the same mistake that your mother and Mary were guilty of.'

After coffee, they walked for a while along the riverbank, listening to the hectic stridulation of the cicadas and breathing in the scent of the wild herbs crushed beneath their feet.

'I love it here,' Holly said at last.

'The temptation to linger is almost

overwhelming. But I'll bring you back. I promise.' She raised her head and turned to him, startled by the rare texture to his voice.

In that moment, when the cicadas were suddenly silent, when her heart held its beat, Holly knew he was going to kiss her. Knew without doubt that she wanted him to kiss her. She turned so easily into his arms and lifted her face, offering herself to him. His mouth was warm, gentle, a kiss between friends, not lovers. Yet when he raised his head, just for that moment she could have sworn that his eyes flared with a sharp desire. But he turned abruptly and said, 'We'd better be getting back. We have an early start tomorrow.'

★　★　★

Holly had thought that it would be a relief to get away from the brightness of the southern sun, but as they descended into the grey cloud blanketing London she pulled a rueful face.

'It's raining,' she said.

'Is it?' Joshua glanced up briefly from a sheaf of papers that had apparently needed his undivided attention throughout the flight. 'It won't last.'

After the almost dream-like quality of their evening together, when all problems had seemed suspended in a mixture of sights and scents heightened by his presence, the morning had brought Holly back to earth with a bump. Joshua had appeared in the early morning, hollow-cheeked as if he had not slept much, refusing anything but coffee. He had been almost sharp with her and clearly not disposed to talk.

He whisked them through Passport Control and Customs with practised ease and his car was waiting at the kerb, a chauffeur ready to open the door for her and deal with her luggage.

'There's no need to take me home, Joshua,' she said quickly, anxious to get away from his disturbing presence and put herself back into a more everyday frame of mind. 'I can easily catch a bus.' Last night was clearly as embarrassing in recollection to him as it was to her. He had only kissed her because she had practically thrown herself into his arms and she had no wish to be reminded of her own foolishness. But he was apparently unmoved by her protest.

'Don't be silly; just get in.'

'David would come — '

'I'm sure he would.' Holly felt her cheeks grow warm under his provoking gaze. 'Or you could even take a cab, but since I insist on taking you home there's not much point in a prolonged discussion of the alternatives.' He held the car door, his look suggesting that they had been standing on the kerb for quite long enough. She climbed into the back of the Rolls without another word, quite unable to explain that she didn't want to sit by him, feel the warmth of his shoulder next to hers and know that he would be quite unmoved by the experience.

The car moved smoothly into the traffic, through the underpass and on to the motorway. He had been right about the weather. Already the sky was clearing and the sun was breaking through to light the distant, familiar view of Windsor Castle. She would soon be home, facing up to this new life. But without Joshua, she thought, there would be no great pleasure in it.

As they approached the junction where they should turn off the chauffeur moved out into the fast lane and accelerated to clear a line of lorries.

Holly frowned. 'I think we've just missed my turning.' She turned to Joshua. 'This isn't the way home.'

'Isn't it?' His eyes asked a question of her and, under their unwavering grey power, she found herself confused and unable to offer a coherent answer. She stared down at her fingers busily pleating the cloth of her jeans.

'Ashbrooke isn't my home.'

'It could be.' For a moment his eyes offered her a glimpse of hope, yet she hesitated, unwilling to make a fool of herself again.

'I don't think so.'

'Then the sooner you get this over with, Holly, the better,' he advised impassively, and she knew she had been right. 'Have you any idea what you will do with yourself now?' he asked. 'Have you made any plans?'

'No,' she said, making an effort to appear cheerful. 'I suppose that's why I stayed away so long. I've nothing to come home for.'

'Not even David?'

She turned to him. Was that why he had held back last night? 'Not even David,' she said. Then, afraid that she had betrayed herself, she lifted her shoulders. 'At least I won't have to paint 'bread-and-butter' pictures any more.'

'I think you could safely say that.'

'It's a lot simpler that way. Absolute freedom requires a great deal more discipline. And I'm going to miss teaching.'

'What about all the stuff you've been doing in Italy and France?' he asked. The memory of the way his brows had shot up at the weight of her portfolio provoked a smile.

'Some of it is good, I think. I'll have to look at it in the cold light of day. But I feel I'd like to do something different. Something quite new. I always wanted to . . . ' She hesitated to expose herself to his ridicule.

'Go on,' he pressed, and she found herself telling him about a visit to the studio of a sculptor she had met in Florence and her interest in trying this, for her, very different form. He encouraged her to elaborate and the miles had flown by before she recalled that she was supposed to be annoyed with him for taking her to Ashbrooke.

'Are you hungry?' he asked after a while. 'Or can you wait until we get home?'

'I'd prefer to wait.'

The weather continued to clear as they drove westwards and by the time they approached Ashbrooke there were only a few clouds to break up the eggshell-blue of the sky and the sun was striking warm through the car window.

'We'll call at the house first,' Joshua offered in explanation as they passed the hotel entrance. 'It won't take long.'

'Fine,' she said, her careless tone covering a rising feeling of something between panic and excitement, and she almost held her breath as they turned and swept along the coast road to Highfield.

When they arrived she climbed out of the car and looked around her. She had barely had time to register the scale of the grounds on the day of the funeral. The garden near the house was cultivated with the sort of careless charm that required far more effort than neat beds to achieve. But above them and along the low cliff the land had been left wild.

'I can't believe just how lovely it is here.'

'Yes,' Joshua agreed. 'We'd better get

on, Holly. I simply need some decisions about the disposal of the furniture,' he interrupted her contemplation.

'Is it that urgent?' she asked, thinking how good it would be simply to walk for a while on the soft, new grass.

'If you sign the contract in the morning, we can wrap everything up the same day. Since you're so anxious to leave.' Holly was in no hurry to go home to deal with David and broken guttering and a pile of other tedious things. Now she was in Ashbrooke, she thought she might stay on for a few days. His suggestion that everything could be dealt with so quickly astonished her.

'You mean everything? Do everything tomorrow?' It hardly matched the long-drawn-out problems that her friends had encountered when buying and selling property.

'I told you,' he said. 'We've just been waiting for you to turn up and sign the contract.'

'And if I hadn't returned with you today?' she asked.

He apparently hadn't considered such a possibility, but he humoured her. 'The company that wants to buy would have waited a few more days, I suppose. They're very keen.'

'A company wants to buy Highfield?' She frowned. 'As a home for one of their staff?' she asked.

'You won't get a better offer,' he said. 'They've been after Mary to sell to them for a couple of years.'

'But she wouldn't?' He didn't answer, but she persisted. 'You'd better tell me exactly what they plan to do here.'

There was something measuring about the cool grey eyes. 'Why do you want to know, Holly? You've made it quite clear that you won't want to stay here.'

'So I should take the money and run; is that what you're telling me to do? You'd better give it to me straight, Joshua, or I won't be signing anything. Who are they?'

He hesitated for a moment, then shrugged. 'Ashbrooke Leisure.' He gave it to her 'straight', making no effort to sweeten the planned development or suggest that it was especially undesirable. 'It's the usual sort of thing. They plan to extend the house and turn it into a club, put a games complex and indoor pool over there and there'll be caravans along here and up there.'

'Caravans?' she said, shocked. 'How many?'

'Two hundred,' he said. 'So I believe.'

She looked around her and saw the unspoilt countryside and wondered what a couple of hundred caravans would do to it. 'What about planning permission?' she asked. 'Surely they haven't a hope — '

'They have it already.' He saw her raised eyebrows and explained. 'You don't have to own land to apply for planning permission to build on it, or change its use.'

'And they got it? Just like that?'

He was getting a little impatient. 'There were a few objections,' he admitted.

'I'll bet. No wonder they're so

anxious to get on with the purchase,' she said thoughtfully. 'They've gone to a lot of trouble.'

His mouth hardened. 'And expense. If you're thinking of trying to push up the price I would urge you to reconsider.'

'I don't believe you've mentioned the price.' He did and an involuntary gasp escaped her lips. No wonder he hadn't softened the blow. She could hardly blame him for thinking she could be bought for what was undoubtedly a great deal of money. But was it enough for such a site? Her brows furrowed in thought. 'Did they offer — ?'

'Mary wouldn't even talk to them, but this was her home. She'd always lived here. I don't believe that any amount of money would have made her move.' The implication being that Holly would sell because she didn't care?

She shaded her eyes against the sun as she looked westwards along the coast. What would two hundred caravans do to the view? she wondered unhappily. Nothing, if you kept your eyes firmly out to sea. She spotted a campsite in the distance. Someone had already made themselves at home. 'Who are they?' she asked.

He turned to look. 'That's a special campsite for children and young people, part of the holiday programme organised by the Graham Foundation. Mary's charity.'

'The one you helped her to found?'

'I gave her financial advice, that's all.'

'And what will happen to that campsite when I sign your piece of paper?'

He threw her a sharp glance. 'Does it matter?' he asked. She didn't bother to dignify this with a reply, simply waited, hands on hips, for him to answer her question. He shrugged carelessly. 'I imagine it would have to go. It's right by the access point to the beach.' He turned away quickly. 'Shall we go inside? I'd like to get on with the furniture.'

''Imagine'?' Holly echoed, suddenly very angry. 'Don't you know? Don't you care? I'm an outsider, but you live

150

in Ashbrooke. It's your home.' Or was he getting ready to take the money and run as well? He'd said something about selling the Hall. She shivered as a cold hand feathered her spine. Just how deeply involved in this deal was Mr Joshua Kent? Could it be that it was the reason he had befriended Mary in the first place, why he had taken so much trouble to come and fetch her, Holly, from France, had taken so much trouble to disarm her? At least he hadn't been able to bring himself to actually seduce her. She felt a hot flush of shame as she realised how easy it would have been. 'Well?' she demanded, ignoring the sick feeling that threatened.

His face was impassive. 'It would have to go.'

'Show me,' she demanded.

'I should have thought you would be rather tired,' he objected.

'Tired?' she repeated dully. Too tired after the flight and the long drive down here to be able to think clearly? She was beginning to wonder if he had been going to produce the contract the moment they returned to the hotel, ready to be signed while she still had her head full of Dresden shepherds and Sheraton whatnots. 'Not at all. I'm beginning to feel the need for some good, fresh air.' She lowered her lashes. 'But you get on with listing the furniture if you like,' she said, making her voice kind to suggest subtly that a walk might be a bit too much for him. She didn't wait for his reaction, but set off across the garden and along a clearly marked footpath towards the campsite.

She had gone barely twenty yards before he was alongside her. She glared at him.

'I thought I might just manage it,' he said, attempting to lighten the atmosphere. 'If you took my arm . . . '

'It's a public footpath,' she threw back at him, avoiding his hand at her elbow, a little stab of anger spilling over into her voice.

She walked swiftly along the path, making it clear enough that she had no further interest in conversation. It took most of fifteen silent minutes before they reached the campsite and she was the breathless one.

'This way.' The path dipped sharply and he took her arm as she slithered down the slippery grass to the lower level where the camp was set up. Here the cliff dipped almost to the beach and it was easy enough to scramble down on to the sand, but wide steps had been constructed and a shallow ramp down to a wooden deck for anything on wheels. She walked down the steps, running her hands down the smooth rail, appreciating the thought that had gone into the design.

'Did the Foundation pay for this work?' she asked, turning to him.

'Yes.'

'It must have cost a great deal of money. Will your developers reimburse it, or am I expected to repay it out of the proceeds of the sale?'

'I expect we can work something out,' he said. Her all too obvious anger seemed to amuse him and that made it ten times worse.

'Then it had better be before the contracts are signed, don't you think?'

'You're learning very quickly, Holly.'

'Am I?' she asked, with apparent surprise. 'It just seems like common sense to me. I'm surprised you didn't think of it yourself.'

He took a deep breath and bit back whatever retort had leapt to his tongue. 'Do you want to see anything else?' he asked politely. 'There is a shower- and toilet-block tucked away in those trees.'

'Oh, I want to see everything, Joshua,' she assured him forcefully. And it was true; she did. Every inch of Mary's home. Every blade of grass. Every tree.

Joshua led the way to where a group of youngsters were playing games under the watchful supervision of their leaders.

One of them came hurrying over, smiling broadly, and then stopped quite suddenly. 'Good lord,' she said as she caught sight of Holly. 'You gave me quite a turn. I thought you were Mary's ghost.'

'This is her cousin, Holly Carpenter. She owns the land now,' Joshua said quickly.

'Laura Marsden,' said the woman, introducing herself, adding, 'You're very alike, for cousins.' Holly firmly ignored Joshua's eye as Laura expressed her condolences. 'We bring a group of children from London every year. They wouldn't have a holiday if it weren't for the Foundation.' They stood for a moment and watched the children taking part in an obstacle race which involved large quantities of water and a great deal of laughter.

'Holly,' Joshua intervened. 'Time's getting on.'

She smiled sweetly at him. 'There's plenty of time, Joshua. As much time as I need.' Her eyes challenged him to deny it.

Then she turned to say goodbye to the camp leader, who said, 'Why don't you come along to the campfire supper tomorrow evening? We'd love to have you.'

'I'd love to come,' Holly said immediately. 'And if there's anything you need, please don't hesitate to get in touch with me.'

'You're staying up at Highfield?'

There was the smallest pause, with Holly very conscious of Joshua's eyes burning into her back. 'Yes, Laura. I'm staying at Highfield.'

6

Joshua was silent on the walk back, his face expressionless, but Holly told herself she didn't care how angry he was. She wasn't about to be rushed into selling her house to a group of developers who only cared about their profits.

Back at the house he unlocked the door and let her in. Holly was in the living-room before she realised he hadn't followed her. She walked back into the hall. He was standing in the entrance, tossing her keys in his hand.

'Aren't you coming in?' she asked. 'I thought you were determined to sort out the furniture.' She couldn't resist this opportunity to provoke him a little.

'I'm afraid I've run out of time today. I'll come back for you in a couple of hours.'

'Back for me? Damn you, Joshua

Kent. Will you stop trying to run my life? There's no need for you to come back for me.' She glared at him. 'I'm staying here.'

'Then you have a slight problem. There's no food in the house and it's quite a way to the town.'

'A walk won't kill me.'

'No,' he agreed. 'But you won't make it before the shops shut.'

'Oh.'

He took pity on her. 'There's a car in the garage. If you'd like me to I'll arrange some insurance, then you'll be able to do exactly what you like. But if you want to eat tonight I suggest you come up to the Hall.' He didn't wait for her answer, his sudden grin absolutely infuriating, but he returned to the car before she could tell him so. He returned a few moments later with her bag and portfolio.

'Thank you,' she offered a little stiffly.

'You're sure you'll be all right here on your own?' he asked.

She lifted her chin. 'Why on earth

shouldn't I be?' If she hadn't been starving she would have told him what to do with his dinner. But she was only too aware that it had been a long time since lunch on the plane and she hadn't eaten much of that.

He nodded, apparently satisfied. 'Then I'll see you later.'

Despite Holly's bold assertion that she would be fine, it still felt rather odd to be quite alone in a strange house where everything had been left just as if the occupant were about to return — the beds made, towels in the bathrooms, new soap waiting to be used . . . Mary's clothes still hanging in the wardrobe.

She wandered about, not quite knowing what to do, jumping at every unexpected sound made by an old house settling after a warm day.

Her assertion that she would be staying at Highfield had been made on the spur of the moment. She had expected Joshua to try and talk her out of spending any time there, but he hadn't. Maybe he thought that being alone all night in a strange house would sufficiently unnerve her that she would meet him on the doorstep in the morning, bag packed, begging to be taken to Ashbrooke Hall. He would be disappointed. Sleeping on her own in an otherwise empty house was something she was used to.

She decided to sleep in the main guest bedroom. It seemed appropriate; she felt like a guest, after all — a welcome guest, but not quite at home. It was a lovely room, the wallpaper covered with tiny pink rosebuds that were echoed in the print of the bedcover and matched exactly by plain pink velvet curtains. It had its own bathroom and a small dressing-room with a walk-in wardrobe. It took no time at all to hang up the few clothes she had with her and, that done, she ran a bath and wallowed in the sheer luxury of it.

Despite her assertion that a couple of hours would be plenty of time, she was barely ready when she heard the ring of the bell. She had decided to wear another of her purchases from Gordes. Cool turquoise this time, the princess line emphasising her slender figure, a white cuff skimming across her breasts and broad white straps. She quickly applied the final touch of colour to her lips, checked her hair and smiled with satisfaction at her reflection. She was determined to crush Joshua Kent with the ease with which she had made herself at home.

She picked up the tiny matching jacket and pushed her feet into her sandals, before running down the stairs to throw open the door. But it was the chauffeur standing in the porch.

'Mr Kent has been detained, Miss Carpenter. But he didn't want to keep you waiting, so he asked me to fetch you.'

She bit back her chagrin at being foiled in her plan. It was almost as if he had known. She smiled. 'How kind of him.'

Soon after, the Rolls pulled smoothly into the long drive in front of Ashbrooke Hall, but didn't stop at the front entrance. Instead, Holly was driven around the side and the car halted before an old stable-block. The chauffeur opened the door. 'Mr Kent said to go straight up, miss. The door is open.'

She looked uncertainly at the stone stairway that ran up the outside of the building.

'Up here?'

He nodded and after a moment's hesitation she ran lightly up the steps to a half-open door. 'Well, I thought you should know how things stand.' Joshua's voice drifted to her from inside. 'No. Leave that to me, Marcus.' There was a pause. 'I can handle her — No, it shouldn't be too difficult . . . ' He was apparently speaking to someone on the telephone and Holly found herself in the unenviable position of being an eavesdropper, her cheeks growing warm as she realised that she was the subject of the conversation. She knocked loudly.

Joshua pulled the door open, the receiver still in his hand, and for a moment stared at her.

'I'll call you back in the morning,' he told his caller and replaced the receiver on its cradle. 'Come on in, Holly. I'm sorry I didn't come myself. I've been trying to catch up with the messages left on my answering machine.'

'I seem to be taking up rather a lot of your time,' Holly said a little stiffly.

He was reassuring. 'It's no trouble.'

'Isn't it?' she asked. 'Well, once I've signed your papers you'll be able to get back to your own business.' She managed a smile. 'What exactly is your business, Joshua?' she asked, her casual tone hiding the angry acceleration of her heart-rate. 'I don't believe you've ever said.'

His mouth that had once been so forbidding now seemed to smile almost easily. Holly wasn't sure she liked that any better. At least she knew exactly where she was when he was being insufferable.

But he refused to be drawn. 'That's because I make it a habit never to discuss my business out of the office,' he said. 'Would you like a drink?'

She could hardly dispute this blatant lie without revealing that she had overheard part of his conversation and demanding that he tell her exactly what he had meant. But she was certain she knew that already, and equally certain that he would think of something perfectly innocent to fob her off with.

So she made herself smile, too. 'Thank you. A glass of wine?'

'I'll open a bottle. Come on through to the kitchen while I draw the cork. I hope you don't mind eating here? The food will be exactly the same as in the diningroom at the Hall, but we won't have to put up with a horde of onlookers.'

'Do other people find your eating habits that interesting?' she asked, following him into a roomy kitchen fitted in warm antique pine and with a small round table that seemed to suggest intimate breakfasts for two.

He grinned at her. 'Oh, they're used to me. But you, my dear Holly, are a fairly hot item of gossip.'

Holly stared at him in astonishment. 'Why would anyone want to gossip about me?' she demanded to know.

He selected a bottle of wine from an oversized refrigerator. 'Is this too dry for you?' He held up a bottle of Chardonnay, wonderfully golden in the evening light. She shook her head and he applied the corkscrew with deft precision. 'You're an unknown factor,' he explained in answer to her question. 'You've inherited an important piece of local property. And a pretty girl with a considerable fortune is always a matter of interest, as you'll quickly find out.' He pulled the cork, poured the wine into two glasses and handed one to her. 'Now, what would you like to eat?'

His sudden reversion to the matter-of-fact momentarily threw her. 'When David and I have a take-away it's usually a pizza,' she confessed as she took the menu he offered her.

'Really?' He sounded unsurprised. 'Then I suggest you take this opportunity to spoil yourself. What do you like best? Big fat Dublin Bay prawns? Or Luigi makes a pâté stuffed with truffles that defies description. Or quenelles — '

'Stop!' she cried. 'I shall faint from hunger if you keep that up. It seems forever since I had anything to eat. Let me look.'

He laughed, to reveal a row of even white teeth and, with a flourish, held back a chair for her to sit down. Then he drew up another alongside her to sit close, his arm stretched along the back of her chair, his shoulder brushing hers as he leaned over her to point out some special treat. All the time she was trying to concentrate on the menu she was aware of him. The skin on the inside of his arm was smooth against the coolness of her shoulder and smelled only of him. Warm, masculine. She glanced up at him, her mouth inches from his neck, the strong line of his jaw.

He turned to her.

'Decided?'

'The French mushroom tart,' she said quickly. His face was very close, the grey eyes smiling with an unexpected warmth. 'And . . . ' She faltered. For a moment he didn't move and suddenly his arm around her shoulder made their closeness seem very intimate.

'And?' he prompted gently and her insides suddenly seemed to take on a life of their own over which she had no control.

It took an enormous effort of will to make herself respond. 'I'd like the trout fillet, please.'

'Is that all?' For a moment she thought that perhaps he sensed that it was far from all. That he knew she wanted him to bend those last few inches and kiss her. Kiss her properly. And for a moment she thought he was going to do just that. Instead, after a pause that might have been only a second, might have been forever, he stood up and called the hotel kitchen to place their orders. Then, taking their glasses and the bottle of wine, he led the way into the living-room.

'It'll be a while before the food arrives; we might as well be comfortable.' Despite the rough stone walls the room was wonderfully welcoming. Deep burgundy armchairs, a thick carpet and a fireplace piled with logs and fir cones just waiting for a cool evening and the touch of a match. And at the far end, under a wide picture-window that took full advantage of the view, a table had already been laid for two.

She sank into one of the armchairs and curled her legs beneath her. He stretched out in its pair on the other side of the hearth and smiled.

It was a smile that could break your heart, she thought, and with the thought came a sudden chill. For a moment back there in the kitchen, with his arm around her shoulder, she had forgotten that she was angry with him, certain that he was trying to manipulate her to his own ends. But she made herself smile back.

'You should smile more often, Holly. It suits you.' His voice had a new, velvet texture that seemed to ripple down her spine.

She lowered her lashes. 'I think the same could be said for you, Joshua.' For a moment his face stilled.

Holly relaxed back into the armchair. If Joshua Kent thought that flirtation was the way ' . . . to handle her', that she could be romanced out of High-field, far be it from her to disabuse him. For now.

'Perhaps we ought to start this relationship again, Holly, from the beginning.' Joshua was no longer smiling. 'We seem to have begun very badly.' There was a grave intensity in his expression that made it almost impossible to believe that he was simply leading her on. But, as long as she remembered that that was exactly what he was doing, she would be quite safe.

'On the contrary, Joshua. I think

you've been doing rather well,' she answered with equal gravity, relieved that he would take the betraying colour staining her cheeks for something other than indignation that he thought her so gullible. 'So far,' she added softly under her breath.

Joshua's forehead creased in the slightest frown and she thought for a moment that she had gone too far. She had little experience of flirting at this unspoken level of intensity. Her relationships with the opposite sex had been enjoyable, but strictly of the light-hearted kind.

But he leaned across and refilled her glass, his eyes never leaving her face. 'I'm glad, Holly. We should be friends.'

'Friends?' She experimented with a soft laugh.

The bottle slipped through his fingers, hitting the hearth rather hard. 'How long are you thinking of staying there?'

'I'm not sure,' she said airily. 'You were right. I've nothing to rush home for and I'd like to see a little of the countryside round here. Do you think the purchasers will mind waiting a while longer?' She looked him straight in the eye. 'You could always tell them you couldn't find me.'

'And who shall I say is living at the house?' He eyed her thoughtfully, then shrugged. 'You could always move up here.'

'Up here?' she repeated faintly, and felt the slow, betraying spread of heat in her cheeks.

The corners of his mouth creased in the slightest smile. 'To the hotel. I've no idea how long they'll wait, but you do run the risk of losing the sale altogether.'

She ducked her head and tried to cover her confusion by taking a sip of wine. It took a moment for the catch in her throat to release itself. 'After they've taken so much trouble? Waited so long? Surely not,' she objected. 'And I'd prefer to stay at Highfield.'

'It's up to you, but it is my duty to

warn you of the risk. There's always someone else willing to sell, Holly.'

'In Ashbrooke?' she countered.

His forehead creased thoughtfully. 'Perhaps not in Ashbrooke,' he admitted.

Holly was finding it increasingly difficult to maintain her pose under his unrelenting scrutiny. She swallowed, hard. 'Can you see the house from here?' she asked, and without waiting for an answer she stood up and crossed to the window. Joshua followed her.

'It's over there.' He took her shoulders and gently moved her round and, standing close behind her, directed her to the furthest point visible from the window. 'You can just see the rooftop.' His hands remained on her shoulders, the touch of his fingers electric against her bare skin, the length of his body hard against her back. She remained perfectly still, aware that things were moving far more quickly than she had intended.

'Turn round, Holly.' His voice vibrated against her scalp, charging the fine down on her cheek, making every nerve-end hyper-sensitive, so that she was aware of the heat of his body, the steady thud of his heart against her spine.

She turned quickly, a laugh ready to tease away any expectations, but the words died on her lips as his hands slid down to her waist and he drew her close against him and, quite without warning, she was no longer cool. No longer in control.

'What are you doing, Holly?' he demanded roughly.

'Doing?' she breathed.

'You know exactly what I mean. Or do I have to show you?'

Breathing was quite suddenly impossible as she caught the full impact of a mouth ready to take hers by storm.

'Well?' he murmured. She had been an idiot to think that she could outplay someone like Joshua Kent. He wasn't some ordinary small-town man of her own age. She had little doubt that he was an experienced man of the world. And she wasn't a child who could expect to flirt and run. There was only one way he would interpret her behaviour. She had been a fool and had to move, now, quickly, before it was too late. But her legs wouldn't obey her, or perhaps they knew better than she did what she wanted. Her tongue nervously moistened her lips as his head began to descend and she closed her eyes to obliterate the sight of his eyes, smoky with desire, to hide from the knowledge that she no longer cared about his motives.

It was a tap at the door that saved her. For a desperate moment she thought he was going to ignore it as they remained perfectly still, arched together, his lips an inch from hers. Then with an enormous effort of will he straightened, steadying her momentarily.

'I forgot the first rule of the game, Holly.' His voice was ragged, his smile a little crooked. 'If you're going to make love to a woman before dinner, it's wise to cook it yourself.' When he was certain that she could stand, he moved unhurriedly across the room and opened the door. A young waiter from the hotel smiled at her and began to serve their meal. Joshua held a chair for her and she sank into it gratefully, hardly able to support herself.

'This looks wonderful,' she said, when she had regained sufficient control of her vocal cords to speak. Her fork fell through the pastry and she gratefully used the food to avoid eye contact, although she didn't taste a thing. He had as good as admitted that he had intended to seduce her and she had been more than happy to help him. Joshua himself made no attempt to draw her into conversation. He, too, seemed reluctant to break the silence.

The waiter returned after a short while to clear their plates and serve the trout. She sipped nervously at the wine, keeping her eyes focused on the distant view.

After the waiter had gone, Holly picked up her fork, but then she realised that he hadn't moved, was sitting perfectly still watching her. She reluctantly forced herself to meet his eyes. 'What is it?'

'You won't do that again unless you mean it, will you, Holly? It's liable to get you into trouble.'

Her cheeks flamed with embarrassment and something more. Anger, too. There was a dangerous sparkle in her eyes as she said, 'I think I can safely promise that. If you will do the same.'

The split-second flash of surprise that crossed his face gave her a small measure of satisfaction. But when he replied his voice was devoid of emotion.

'You have my assurance, Holly, that the next time I kiss you you'll be left in no doubt of my meaning.' He picked up a fork and gestured with it. 'Now eat your food; it's getting cold.'

She did as she was bid, hardly able to take in what he was saying as he crisply explained that he had arranged temporary insurance for her to drive Mary's car. 'They'll send a form for you to sign in a day or two. I swore you'd never had an accident,' he said and looked up. 'I hope I'm right.'

She suddenly realised that he was expecting some response. 'I've never had an accident. Although it would be difficult to tell from the state of my car. It's held together by will-power.'

'In that case you might find this one rather exciting.' He looked thoughtful, but there was a glint of mischief in his eyes. 'Perhaps you should trade it in for something a little less exacting.'

She bristled. She might not have had a great deal of experience driving, but she was perfectly competent. 'I think I should be the judge of that.'

He shook his head. 'Do you always do the opposite of what you're advised?'

'It depends upon the advice,' she retorted swiftly.

'Then in future I'll be extremely cautious about offering any, but if you need any help just give me a call.'

'I thought you'd be rushing back to London.'

'Not for a day or two. I've a few things to clear up here.'

There it was again, the sharp jab of

suspicion. He had seen through her stupid attempt at sophisticated flirtation and crushed it without raising a sweat. In fact, he was too clever by half. But she had a good idea what he was planning to 'clear up' and she had every intention of thwarting him.

'Would you like something else?' he said, interrupting the flow of her thoughts.

She shook her head. 'No, thanks. That was delicious.'

'Any time,' he said, casually.

'No. Next time it must be my treat. I'll ask you to Highfield for a meal as soon as I've found out how everything works.' A reminder that she planned to stay for as long as she wished. 'Although I can't pretend to compete with this sort of food.' If she hoped to needle him, she did not succeed.

'I look forward to it. Coffee, then, and a brandy?' He smiled. 'No, I remember; you don't like brandy. Come and have a look in the cupboard. There must be something you'd like.'

'No.' She made a move to leave. She

needed to get away from Joshua Kent, get herself back on an even keel. When he was in the same room she found it difficult to think straight. 'Thank you for a lovely meal, but I must go.'

'Must you?' She was certain he was teasing her now.

'It's been a long day.'

'Then I'll take you home.'

'There's no need to bother yourself, Joshua. Your chauffeur is quite up to the task.'

'My chauffeur has finished for the night. Besides, I reserve the pleasure of driving beautiful young women home for myself.'

He held the tiny jacket for her and managed somehow, without touching her at all, to make her feel as if she was being stroked. Or maybe, she thought, it was all in her head. Maybe she just wanted to be stroked by him. If that was the case, he had won the first round by a country mile and she would be far safer retreating while she could. But that would be far too easy a victory.

She owed it to Mary to find out just what was going on.

Fifteen minutes later the car drew up outside the long, low house and Joshua escorted her to the door and unlocked it for her. 'Thank you, Joshua.'

'I'd ask you what you were thanking me for, if I were sure you knew.' He stepped back. 'I'll ring you tomorrow to organise a time to get the probate papers signed.'

'Fine, but don't leave it too late. I have some shopping to do.' He raised his hand and turned away. 'Joshua!'

He turned back. 'Yes?'

She stretched out her hand. 'I think those are my keys.'

He looked down at the bunch of keys in his hand. 'So they are. Force of habit.' He put the keys into the palm of her hand, wrapped her fingers around them and held them there for a moment. 'Keep them safe.'

'I will,' she said. 'You can be quite sure of that.'

She thought for a moment that he

was going to say something else, but instead he raised her hand to his lips and kissed the fingertips where they curled protectively over the keys. 'Goodnight, Holly. Sleep well.'

★　★　★

The sound of the telephone dragged her from sleep. She groped for the phone, confirmed in her belief that they were a curse on mankind.

'Hello?' she mumbled.

'You said to call you early.' The laughter in his voice was an added insult. She opened her eyes sufficiently to look at her watch and groaned.

'Beast!' she said.

'If you don't get up right now you're going to miss the sun. There's rain moving in.'

'If I need a weather forecast I'll look at a piece of seaweed, thanks all the same.'

'How do you think I get my information? Did you sleep well?'

'I *was* sleeping very well, thank you.

What was your problem?'

'No problem at all. I'm going fishing. Before you turn over and go back to sleep, will you make a note to meet me at eleven-thirty this morning in Marcus Lynton's office? It's in the square, opposite the bank. You can't miss it.'

Suddenly wide awake, she sat up, determined to let him know how things stood. 'Joshua, about the house — '

'Sorry, sweetheart, we'll have to leave that for a few days. You've caused a bit of a stir with your enquiry about reparation to the Foundation. I did warn you.'

'So you did,' she said. 'Silly me.' She stuffed the corner of the quilt in her mouth to keep from laughing out loud.

'You said it. See you later.'

'Goodbye, Joshua. Enjoy your fishing.' She dropped the receiver back on to the cradle and threw back the bedclothes, so thoroughly wide awake now that there was no point in staying in bed.

Whether it had been Joshua's instruction to sleep well, or the sound of the sea lulling her to sleep, Holly felt wonderful.

She pulled back the curtains and the approaching rain did nothing to dampen her spirits. She showered and dressed in jeans and a cream Viyella shirt and discovered to her delight that the milkman had been and left a small carton of groceries. Everything she would need for breakfast. And she had no doubt who had asked him to call. She offered up a silent thank-you to Joshua, the temporary halt to the sale putting him back in her good books.

But breakfast could wait. She made her way across the courtyard to a block of outbuildings that contained the garage.

She opened the door and stood for a moment in silent wonder as she took in the sleek black lines of the Lotus sports car. An Elan. Not new. Nowhere near new. But it had been cherished and it was love at first sight.

She sat in the driving seat and soaked in the atmosphere of the car. The smell of old leather, the feel of the wheel, the gear-stick under her hands. She slid the key into the ignition and, her heart pounding, she fired the engine.

There was the most glorious, throaty purr and, almost laughing out loud for the sheer pleasure of it, Holly put the car into reverse and backed it out through the garage doors. An hour later, she and the car were firm friends. She had driven around the yard for a while, making sure of the controls, then along the lane that led out of Ashbrooke. Finally, when she was sure of herself, she had taken the car on to the dual carriageway, quiet so early in the morning, and just enjoyed driving something so beautiful.

After breakfast she drove into the town to find Ashbrooke just opening its doors. She wandered around, looking at the shops, and found herself addressed by name wherever she went. Joshua had not exaggerated when he had said she was the object of local interest. No one actually asked her what her intentions were, but she sensed their curiosity and for the first time wondered what the local people would feel about caravans sprouting like a rash along the clifftop.

She drove home deep in thought, put away her groceries and then, with a sigh, decided that she couldn't put off phoning David any longer.

She called his office and listened for a moment to his ironic thanks for letting him know where she was. 'When are you coming home?' he demanded. 'You've a pile of mail a foot high.'

'I'll be here for a while. Can you send on anything that looks important?'

'If you like,' he said sulkily. 'I suppose you're with Kent?'

'That's really none of your business, David.'

'He'll hurt you, Holly. I'm warning you.' Too late for that, she thought unhappily. 'Not that there's much in the papers these days. He's a very private man.'

'You've been making enquiries about him?' she asked, shaken that David had taken her imagined defection so personally. She had never given him any encouragement. There was an awkward little silence. 'David?' she demanded.

'When he turned up at the house I made it my business to make a few enquiries.' She didn't say anything. 'There's some old money, inherited wealth from his mother's side of the family. But there's a lot more of it these days. Mr Kent is very astute.'

'Oh? What does he do?'

'Anything that makes money.' Her heart sank. It wasn't want she wanted to hear. 'Holly?'

'There's really no need to worry about me, David.' She made herself sound cheerful. 'He's my cousin's executor, that's all. Obviously I should be taking his advice very seriously.'

'What advice?'

'There's a company, Ashbrooke Leisure. They want to buy my house for some holiday development.'

'That sounds serious money. But that's Joshua Kent for you. It seems to stick to him.'

7

Holly neatly reversed the Lotus into a space in front of Joshua's silver Rolls a minute before eleven-thirty. She climbed out and paused briefly to admire her handiwork.

'Very professional.' She jumped as Joshua took her arm and turned her towards Marcus Lynton's office.

'Where did you spring from?' she demanded.

'I had to pick up some share certificates from the bank over there and you arrived just as I came out. I've been standing on the other side of the square watching you.' His eyes creased into a teasing smile. 'Would it have been more difficult to park if you'd known you had an audience?'

'Certainly not,' she said firmly, lying through her teeth. She had reversed into the space without a second's hesitation, but she was sure that it would have been a very different matter if she had known he was watching. Even the simple task of standing beside him in the street, with his hand under her elbow, his lithe body against her shoulder, made control over her limbs a matter for absolute concentration. Putting one foot in front of the other was a great deal harder.

'How did you find it?' he said, nodding towards the car as he opened the door for her.

'The car?' she asked, pausing in the entrance to the solicitor's office. Then, with a nonchalance that took every ounce of acting ability she possessed, she shrugged and encouraged a wicked little smile to dance on her lips. 'I just opened the garage door, Joshua, and there it was.'

His eyes glinted and a slightly unnerving brow crooked a fraction. 'Knives for breakfast, Holly?'

'No,' she said, and had the grace to blush. 'Eggs. For which I thank you.

And owe you,' she added.

'Your thanks are quite sufficient. Just pay the milkman at the end of the week. Shall we get on?' he suggested, urging her through the door. 'Marcus is expecting us.'

For the next hour, she read apparently endless amounts of legal documents at Joshua's insistence, until her head felt as if it had been stuffed full of cotton wool. But he explained everything carefully and when he was sure she understood he let her sign her name to each of them.

At last it was over and he spent a while longer explaining exactly what her income would be and where it would come from. It was all quite bewildering; her only financial problems in the past had been connected with a lack of money, not what to do with large quantities of the stuff. She felt embarrassed by it. Undeserving.

'It's all invested in pretty sound stock. I'd leave it be for the moment,' Joshua said as they finally left the office.

'Thank you. I will.' His eyebrows rose slightly at such unexpectedly meek acceptance of his advice and she raised her shoulders in a deprecating little shrug. 'I have been told you're very good at making money, Joshua.'

'Have you?' His eyes narrowed. 'And just who have you been discussing me with?' There was no change in his voice, yet she had the uncomfortable feeling that he was absolutely furious.

She raised her eyes to his. 'I haven't been discussing you with anyone, Joshua.' The chill was back, she recognised with a sinking heart, the steely eyes wintry in an emotionless face. 'I was simply told that you were astute,' she said, trying to improve matters. It didn't.

'The difference is a little too subtle for me, Holly, but I'll say this for him — David Grantham isn't quite as stupid as I thought.' He nodded abruptly and without another word got into his car and drove away, missing her rear bumper by not much more than a hair's breadth.

'Damn!' How could she have been such an idiot? There had been no need for him to take so much trouble over her affairs. No doubt there were people who would happily pay to have his investment advice and in one thoughtless second she had given him the impression that she hadn't trusted him.

The word twisted inside her. The truth of the matter was that she hadn't trusted him, but there was nothing to be gained by standing on the pavement worrying about it. She wished she had simply asked Joshua outright whether he was involved in the house purchase. He might not have liked it, he might not even have given her a straight answer, but she wouldn't feel quite so dirty.

'Still here?' She turned as Marcus came up behind her. 'I thought I saw Josh drive away.' Then he smiled as he saw the car. 'Oh, I see. You're driving yourself. Nice little job, isn't she?'

'Lovely,' Holly replied absently, her thoughts still wrapped up in her own foolishness.

'Well, if you're not having a celebration lunch with Joshua, why don't you join me instead? You can tell me all about your plans.'

Holly turned to the slight, white-haired figure of Marcus Lynton, intending to put him off. She didn't feel particularly like company, certainly not like celebrating. But the smile was full of charm, and on an impulse she said, 'We'll have lunch together, Marcus. But only if it's my treat.'

He laughed. 'In that case, my dear, it will be a double pleasure. Shall we try the White Hart? They do a passable cutlet.' He took her across the square and insisted on buying her a drink, at least.

'I'd better stick to orange juice while I'm driving,' she said, and he fetched their drinks and a menu and, when they were settled at a quiet table in the corner, he asked her how she was settling into Ashbrooke.

'The house is lovely. I haven't seen much of the town yet.'

'Yet? Can we dare hope that you're planning to stay with us for a while?'

'I'd rather like to, but Joshua tells me that the people who want to buy Highfield are pressing for an exchange of contracts. Or they were.' Her smooth forehead creased in concentration. 'I have apparently thrown a spanner into the works.'

'Have you? What've you done?'

'Oh, I just suggested that the buyers should recompense the Graham Foundation for all the work they did at the campsite.'

Marcus looked thoughtful. Took a sip of his drink. 'And what did Josh say to that?' he asked carefully.

'He thought something could be worked out.'

'If he says so, I'm sure it's right. Who are these buyers?'

'Don't you know? I thought there had been some dispute over planning permission for a caravan park.'

Marcus choked on his drink and by the time he had recovered lunch had arrived and for a moment they were occupied with more mundane matters. But Holly reverted to the subject as soon as the waitress had left.

'What do you think of the prospect of a couple of hundred caravans on the cliffs at Highfield, Marcus? Is it a good idea, do you think? Would it provide jobs locally?'

'I can honestly say that I don't know,' he answered evenly and she was certain he was hiding something. 'Perhaps you should ask Josh for a few more details. He seems to know all about it.'

'Yes, Marcus, I think I will.'

'Actually this might be a good time to ask you about the Graham Foundation. There was a meeting of the trustees last week and they were wondering if you could be persuaded to take some active role.' She seemed at a loss. 'Because of the family connection?' he suggested.

Holly's mind was wrenched from contemplation of a cold spot of misery that had unaccountably settled in her chest. 'In what way?'

'Well, Mary took an active part in promoting the Foundation's work. She had a very great love of children, you know. It always seemed a pity that she never married and had children of her own.'

This was so unexpected that she almost blurted out the truth, and Marcus looked at her oddly as she gave a little gasp. 'I'd like to do something,' Holly said quickly, in an effort to hide her confusion. 'In fact, I'm going to have supper tonight with the holiday group camping up at Highfield.'

'That's the spirit. See for yourself what's being done. I'll drop off some of the literature in a day or two and you can have a think about it. There's no great hurry.'

Holly paid the bill and they made their way to the door. The rain that had been threatening all morning had finally begun to fall with a vengeance and they ran together across the square back to her car, where Marcus paused to offer his hand and thank her for lunch, before returning to his office.

She sat for a moment in the dashing Lotus, trying to sort out all the conflicting emotions that were jostling for attention. Marcus had been very odd about the caravan park. He knew something, she was certain. As she started the car, she made herself a solemn promise. Whatever decision she came to about Highfield would be her own. Made with all the facts. She would start making enquiries after the week-end.

*　*　*

The rest of the day went quickly enough, without any further interruptions from Joshua, or anyone else for that matter. For a while she pottered about the house, poking through cupboards, finding little treasures that had belonged to her mother, getting the feel of the place, more at home with every passing hour. Then, when the sun unexpectedly broke through the grey, she put on a pair of wellingtons and an old waxed jacket she found hanging in the rear porch and went outside.

Even drenched with the rain the garden was lovely and she wandered about the narrow paths, coming across unexpected delights tucked in odd corners. A beautiful white Lutyens garden seat set to take advantage of a glimpse of the sea through a stone archway. A tiny burble of water, bubbling through a ring of old granite setts. A delicate little statue of Aphrodite glistening with rain and looking as if she had just that moment stepped from the sea.

She followed the path as it wound mysteriously through a shrubbery until she came to a brick building that might once have been a store of some kind, the front almost overgrown now with a pale pink flush of clematis. Holly tried the door, but it was locked and she fished in her pocket for her bunch of keys.

She eventually found one that turned

in the lock. She hesitated for just a moment before she opened the door, wondering what she would find on the other side. Nothing but dust and cobwebs probably and she shuddered at the thought. But she had to know and, impatient with herself for being so foolish, she turned the handle and threw it open.

Then for a long time she just stood there in the doorway and tried to take in what was before her. It was a studio. Fresh, new canvases by the dozen were stacked against the opposite wall. On shelves there were tubes of paint laid out in every colour, oils and water-colours and pots of gouache. There were brushes, palettes, an easel with a blank canvas propped against it, inviting her to start immediately on some major work, somehow waiting for her to open the door and find it. She took a step forward and was lost. How could she ever leave this wonderful place?

She had promised herself that what-ever decision she made about the house would be hers, but Mary had taken it out of her hands. There was no longer a decision to be made. She was staying.

She locked up carefully and made her way back to the house. As she opened the door she heard the telephone ringing, but it stopped before she could reach it and she shrugged, unconcerned. After this morning it wasn't likely to be Joshua and whoever else might want her would certainly ring again.

She twisted her hair into a French plait, put on a clean pair of jeans and a thick sweater. There was a pair of stout lace-up boots in the back porch. She and Mary had the same size feet and she thought they would be more comfortable than wellingtons to wear for the cook-out. But she decided to wear the waxed jacket; the rain hadn't gone very far.

As she walked along the clifftop the sound of excited voices reached her and she smiled. She would phone Marcus in the morning and tell him she would do whatever she could for the Foundation. And ask him how she could protect the land from marauding developers.

Those decisions taken, she felt her step lighten and the eager swoop of children around her carried her through to the fireside. She handed the bags of goodies she had brought to be shared out among them to Laura. 'I probably shouldn't have brought sweets, but I didn't know what else to bring.'

'They don't get that many; it's a genuine treat for them.' Laura eyed her thoughtfully, then after a moment said, 'Come and give us a hand with the barbecue, if you like.'

'I should have brought marshmallows to toast,' Holly said, looking regretfully at the fire as they passed.

'Don't worry; Josh was ahead of you. He dropped them off earlier.'

'Joshua?' Was it panic making her heart beat like a trapped bird? Or hope? 'Is he here?'

Laura smiled. 'No, more's the pity. He's great with the kids. But I'm sure he'll get back if he can.'

Holly remembered the woman's welcoming smile when they'd walked up to the site the day before. It hadn't been for her. When Laura had noticed her she'd thought she had seen a ghost. The smile had been for Joshua and somehow that was a shock. Holly tried to analyse the feeling, understand why exactly she should be surprised when, by his own admission, he had helped Mary set up the charity. It made his present behaviour just that bit more incomprehensible.

But, wrapped in a red and white striped apron of vast proportions and wielding a pair of tongs to turn the sausages and burgers deftly, Holly didn't have too much time to dwell on the enigma that was Joshua Kent and she felt thoroughly toasted herself when she finally sank on to a blanket beside the fire.

'I don't suppose by any chance you can play this thing?' Laura asked her, holding out a guitar. 'I've burnt my finger and it makes playing even more impossible than usual.'

'Well,' Holly said doubtfully, 'I'm no John Williams.'

'Hell, who wants John Williams? If you can strum that's at least a hundred per cent better than me. Off you go.'

'You believe in working a body hard for her supper round here, don't you?' Holly laughed and ran her fingers experimentally over the strings.

'There's no such thing as a free marshmallow, Holly. Not around this campfire.'

The mention of marshmallows brought Joshua sharply to mind and just as sharply she pushed the image away. She didn't want to think of him, or his perilous grey eyes.

'What do they know?' she asked.

'Not a lot. Start with something simple and they'll soon catch on. They're pretty bright.'

Holly thought for a moment, strummed a chord and began to sing 'London's Burning'. With Laura's encouragement the children soon caught on to the idea of singing in rounds and as the evening progressed her memory obligingly provided a continuous stream of action songs from her days camping with the Guides. They were so noisily enthusiastic that she was unaware of the approach of a dark figure across the grass until the children's voices gradually petered out and she turned around to look.

She didn't actually scream and for that fact alone she would be forever grateful as the black-leather-clad figure removed his helmet and Joshua stared down at her.

'Having a good time?' The leap of excitement that his nearness inevitably seemed to evoke was immediately quashed by the coolness of his voice. He hadn't forgiven her. Why should he? And she would do well to remember that he had his own reasons for making himself useful to her. She lowered the temperature of her voice to match his.

'Yes, thank you.'

Laura moved aside to let him in

alongside her and offered him a drink. 'I'm afraid cocoa is the best I can offer, Josh.'

'That'll do fine. I hope you've saved me a marshmallow to melt on top.' Laura grinned and departed and Joshua sank down into the space she had vacated.

In an attempt to ignore him, Holly struck a chord and began to play again, but most of her mind was riveted on the man beside her, divesting himself of his jacket. Suddenly her fingers were all over the place and without a word Joshua reached across and took the guitar from her lifeless hands.

'What do you want to sing?' he demanded of the children.

They all shouted back something different.

He put his hand to his ear. 'What did you say?' Each time they shouted he pretended he couldn't hear them and they loved him for it. Holly watched as he egged them on, thinking that he would be very easy to love.

He had them almost hysterical with excitement before he raised his hands for silence and in seconds it would have been possible to hear a pin drop, if anyone was interested. Then he began to play something quiet and simple that they all seemed to know and in a minute the children's voices were lifted against his surprisingly good baritone.

For a moment she listened, until she picked up the words of the old folk song and then joined in. Looking at their faces in the firelight, hearing the sounds of the voices against the backdrop of the sea, was an almost magical experience, one Holly knew she would remember forever. She glanced at the profile of the man beside her, dark against the late evening sky. Whether the magic was the moment itself, or because he turned just then and smiled at her quite unexpectedly, she couldn't be certain.

As they finished, Laura and the other helpers arrived with trays of cocoa for the children and then they trailed sleepily off to bed. Holly offered to help, but Laura told her to stay put and the two of them were left alone beside the dying embers of the fire.

'I didn't know you had a motorbike,' Holly said after a while. 'It doesn't seem to quite fit the image.'

'Perhaps you're looking at the wrong image. There's a lot you don't know about me, Holly Carpenter. Why don't you ask your journalist friend to dig a little deeper? Who knows what else he might come up with?' He shrugged as if it was a matter of complete indifference to him one way or the other. 'Besides, I refuse to bring the Rolls down that muddy cart-track.'

'Oh? You weren't so very careful this morning.'

He raised his eyes from the mug in his hand. 'I was extremely careful. I missed your car by at least an inch and a half.'

'Oh, well,' she said, with exaggerated relief. 'That's all right, then.'

'I had every right to be angry.'

206

'I know. And I apologise.'

'Oh, well,' he said, imitating her tone exactly. 'That's all right, then.' Her head came up with a jerk but, to her astonishment, he was laughing.

'Is it?' she asked.

He reached out and touched her lips briefly with his finger. 'Forget it, Holly. I expect I'd have done the same in your shoes.' She wanted to protest, to explain, but that touch had said plainly enough that the subject was closed. 'Come on; I'll take you home.' He pulled her to her feet.

'It's all right; I can walk,' she said quickly.

He looked at her. 'You're not scared of the bike, are you?' No, she thought unhappily, it wasn't anywhere nearly that simple. She wasn't frightened of motorbikes, but if that would do it she was quite prepared to pretend. But it didn't work. Instead of allowing her to go, his fingers tightened around hers. 'There's nothing to it. Come on; you'll love it.'

'But what about a helmet?' she protested.

'I've a spare,' he said, and that, apparently, was that.

They stopped first to say goodnight to Laura and wish them all a safe journey home the next day. 'If you need anything dried before you go, come up to the house. You can put it in the drier,' she offered.

'You're an absolute angel; it must run in the family. I hope you'll be here next year.'

Holly glanced across at Joshua by the bike where he had gone to fetch a helmet for her. 'Thank you, Laura. I hope so too.'

'Ready to go?' Joshua asked as she reached him. Holly nodded and he pulled on the helmet for her and fastened the strap beneath her chin. 'Very fetching. Don't forget to hold tight.' He put on his own helmet and then climbed on to an enormous black machine. She sat very primly behind him, her hands scarcely touching the sides of his waist. Then he started the bike and without further warning moved off and she threw herself at his back and clung on for dear life.

Roaring up the lane, the stab of the headlamp into the dark the only source of light in a black world, was bad. As dreadful as it could be. But it was nothing to do with the noise of the bike, or the speed with which the hedge flashed by them. It was her body pressed against the supple leather of his jacket, feeling the steady, reassuring hammer of his heart against the crazy counterpoint of her own, beating much too fast. It was her arms around his waist, her hands clasped desperately under his ribs. That was what she feared. The unavoidable closeness and what it was doing to her.

Then it was over. They were in front of Highfield and she was sliding quickly from the machine in an effort to escape, her legs wobbly as she had known they would be. She fought desperately with the uncooperative strap of her helmet to remove it before he could help her, touch her. But her fingers couldn't, or wouldn't, find the release and after he had removed his own helmet he bent to do it for her. She shivered.

'Are my hands cold?' he asked.

'No. Yes.' With his long fingers brushing against her neck she couldn't think clearly.

'Well?' he asked, pulling the helmet off and putting it with his own on the seat of the bike then leaning back against it. 'Which is it?'

'They're cold,' she managed before turning quickly away, determined to get inside before she betrayed herself totally. 'Thanks for the lift, Joshua,' she said, from the doorway.

'Holly?' His voice grated against her spine and she stopped and turned slowly back to face him. He hadn't moved.

'Yes?' she asked, from the safe distance of her porch.

'There was something else.'

'Can't it wait?' She fumbled desperately in her pocket for her keys.

'I don't believe it can.' Her margin of safety proved illusory as, in a stride, he was beside her, his eyes smoky dark as he searched her face. It was a look that seemed to touch her, stroke her, burn her up until she thought she would cry out. After a moment, or it might have been an age, in which she felt as if she was suspended at the top of a roller-coaster, waiting for that dizzy, freefall plunge, he spoke. 'I don't believe it can wait another moment.'

She closed her eyes in an effort to blot out the desire in his eyes, not quite trusting it, but knowing that it was far too late for her to fight the echoing response he must all too clearly see in hers. Knowing that she was helpless to resist.

He took her face between his hands, tilting her face upwards and holding it cradled in his long fingers until she could bear it no longer and her long lashes fluttered open. 'Please . . . ' The word, barely more than a sigh, escaped her lips, but whether she was begging

211

for release or capture she scarcely knew. Until he kissed her, and by then it was too late.

His lips were cool as they began to feather her face with butterfly kisses, each touch to the delicately veined lids of her eyes, her temples, the smooth curve of her jaw the gentlest, teasing caress that gradually turned her bones to jelly.

She was trembling as at last he slid his hands inside her jacket, pulled her tight against his chest and held her there.

'What are you doing?' she whispered, her eyes jet-dark in the sudden shaft of moonlight breaking through the clouds.

He laughed, very softly. 'If you have to ask, my darling Holly, I must be doing something wrong.' But he wasn't doing anything wrong; she was quite sure of that. In fact, as his lips continued their philandering progress, she had the very definite impression that he was an expert. Then he raised his head and she moaned very softly.

'Don't stop,' she protested.

'I haven't stopped.' His arm tightened about her waist, drawing her so close along the length of him that suddenly she didn't have any breath for words. And then that was no longer a problem, because she had something else to occupy her mind as his mouth claimed hers and she knew he had spoken nothing but the truth. He left her in absolutely no doubt of his meaning.

Her lips parted under the sensuous prompting of his tongue and she responded with an urgency that at once shocked and elated her, her arms snaking around his neck, pulling him down to her until, with a groan, he wrenched himself free.

His ragged breathing matched her own as they stood just inches apart, staring at one another in stunned amazement at the reality of what had just happened to them both.

'Holly . . . '

She shook her head. It wasn't a time

for words. Her hand fastened on the cold keys in her pocket and she held them for a moment, clenched tight in her fist. Then, her cheeks flushed with bright colour, she extended her hand and offered them to Joshua.

For a heartbeat they hung from the tip of her finger, glinting in the fitful moonlight between the two motionless figures, then he reached out and his fingers closed around them and she surrendered them into his care. He turned to the door, fitted the key in the lock. The sound of the lever drawing back in the mechanism was like the crack of a pistol in the unnatural silence and then the door swung open.

8

Neither of them moved. Holly wasn't even sure that she could. Her legs were planted where she stood, her heart hammering so wildly in her own ears that she was sure Joshua must be able to hear it too and she had apparently lost the power of speech.

But he could not have mistaken her invitation. One look at her would be enough to tell the world that the only thing in the world she wanted at that moment was to be swept up by him and carried away to her rose-covered bed.

His sudden movement took her by surprise and she almost cried out as he stepped back, his rejection stamped in granite features. Every inch of her was weak with the trembling need that had quickened under his searching lips, the turmoil of a desire so urgent that for a moment she thought she might fall.

She didn't fall. Pride insisted that she stiffen her spine and take her pain without flinching. For a moment she steadied herself against the doorpost, found that, despite all expectations to the contrary, her legs would still move, but it was as if in some kind of dream, or nightmare, that she stepped inside and slowly turned to him.

'Goodnight, Joshua.' Her voice caught, grated, didn't quite make the words. She gave up after that. The effort of thanking him for the lift was too much. She just wanted him to go so that she could close the door, forget her pride and sink to the floor.

But he didn't move. He stayed where he was, on the other side of the threshold, his face shadowed, unsmiling, and when he spoke his voice, too, was ragged.

'I shouldn't have done that, Holly. I didn't intend to, God knows. It just happened.' A small moan escaped her lips and she swayed and in a stride he was at her side, her icy hands clasped between his. Then he bent and kissed her, very gently on the lips.

He turned and walked away before she could protest or answer him, pulling on the black helmet with a fierce expression that gave the lie to his devastating self-control. He looked at her just once more before he swung a long, leather-clad leg across the bike, but what was in his eyes was hidden by the dark visor. Then the machine roared into life, shattering the silence, sending an owl swooping in panic across the garden, and for a moment they both watched it. When it had gone they exchanged a look, hers betraying the aching void that his departure was leaving inside her, his nothing but the blank black reflection of his helmet. Then he raised his hand and was gone.

Leaning weakly against the door-frame, she stayed where she was, listening to the changing notes of the engine as it climbed away over the hill, as far as the main road, then it grew fainter and merged with the other sounds of the night.

From somewhere in the garden the scent of an early honeysuckle reached her and she walked for a while, searching for it. But the plant was as elusive as an answer to her confused thoughts. It began to rain again and finally she went inside.

★　★　★

She spent a wakeful night. She didn't toss and turn; she didn't even bother to try to sleep. Instead she allowed her thoughts to wander where they would, but they always came back to the same place. Joshua and her ever-present doubts about his motives. Because if Joshua was the opportunist that she suspected, then why had he walked away from her tonight?

Not because of a lack of desire for her. She hadn't imagined the ardour that had blazed in his eyes the moment before he had stepped back from the brink. And the decision had been entirely his, she knew, and she felt her cheeks burn in the darkness because it had been left entirely to his sense of honour.

And that raised the question of whether she had been entirely wrong about him, because if Joshua was an honourable man he would surely disclose any conflict of interests between his role as Mary's executor and his business dealings.

And there was another question that had been flickering on the edge of her consciousness ever since her doubts had first surfaced. Not urgent enough to batter its way through the intensity of emotion, of confused feelings that had swamped her since her homecoming. But now, as she lay awake, her whole being concentrated on trying to find some answers, it slipped through and was suddenly very loud, very urgent. If Joshua did have something to hide, it asked, why had he insisted she come home?

The sky was beginning to lighten with the silvery promise of a clear day and she threw back the bedclothes, unwilling to stay a moment longer in bed with the unresolved questions going round and round her head. She showered, wrapped herself in a long towelling robe and went downstairs to make some tea.

She took her mug out into the garden and settled herself on the bench as the sun rose behind her, hoping that the fresh air would clear her mind and provide some answers for the endless questions. One question in particular. Why had he wanted her to come home?

He had been so anxious for her to sign the contract to sell the house, had been urging her not to delay in case the purchasers backed out. It all seemed clear enough, cut and dried. But then she kept running into the inescapable fact that if he had allowed her to stay in France she would have quite willingly signed his piece of paper, right there and then, under that olive tree. In fact she had offered to do just that. At the time she would have signed anything to rid herself of his disturbing presence and she would never have known about the caravan site.

And, despite his assertion that there were pressing reasons for her to return with him, there had been no evidence of this since she had come to Ashbrooke. She had signed a load of papers, it was true. But they would have kept. And there had been Marcus Lynton's rather odd reaction to her mention of a caravan park. He hadn't seemed to know anything about it. There was certainly something going on. But quite what she was at a loss to say.

Holly sipped the hot tea. She would tell Joshua today that she had decided against selling. Perhaps his reaction to that news would bring everything into sharper focus.

The sound of someone calling her name filtered through her thoughts. She turned, a slight frown flickering across her brow, and glanced at her watch. It was not quite six. A little early for callers.

'Hello?' she called.

There was a rustling as someone pushed through the slightly overgrown path. 'Holly? Where the hell are you?'

Then she recognised the sharp impatience in the voice and her frown deepened. 'David? What are you doing here?'

He ran a hand over a stubbly chin and grinned. 'That's not a very pleasant welcome, considering I've driven half the night to come and see you.'

'And why on earth would you do that?' she demanded, not at all happy at this unexpected arrival, certain that if David had driven overnight from Berkshire it would only be for his benefit.

'Give me a cup of coffee and I'll tell you.'

'Very well, but you might have phoned.'

'Thus speaks the woman who wouldn't have a telephone in the house at any price.' He glanced at the façade of High-field and pulled a wry face. 'But apparently that's not all that's changed. The 'snags' have all been ironed out, have they?'

She gave an embarrassed little shrug. 'I thought it was all a mistake.'

'Did you? Why?' It was the offhand, casual manner of the question that immediately alerted her to the fact that he sensed a story. There would be a long pause. Someone less wary would fall into it, pouring out their soul rather than listen to the uncomfortable silence.

'Are you coming in?' she asked, and he grinned, quite unashamed at being found out, and followed her into the house.

'I did telephone, by the way. Yesterday afternoon and all evening. Perhaps you should go the whole hog and have an answering machine, now you've finally given up the cleft stick and succumbed to the age of communication.'

'And make things easy for you? Besides, I like the post. People think twice about what they have to say when they have to write.' She led the way through to the kitchen and began to pile bacon on to the grill. 'Tea or coffee?'

'Coffee, please.' He threw an envelope down on the central island. 'I've brought you a few cuttings about your precious Joshua Kent. It's mostly old stuff. I did warn you that he's a very private man.' He plumped himself down on a stool.

'I didn't ask you for them,' she pointed out. 'And why the desperate rush down here yourself? A stamp would have brought them by Monday.'

David looked slightly awkward. 'When I was digging about I stumbled across something. Something I think your Mr Kent will have to talk to me about, whether he likes reporters or not.'

Her hand shook as she cracked an egg into a bowl and the yoke broke. 'Doesn't he like reporters?' she asked, glaring at him. 'I wonder why?'

David didn't seem to notice her sharp, cynical tone. 'I want to ask him about Ashbrooke Leisure.'

'Ashbrooke Leisure?' She hated the glint of triumph in his eyes.

'Exactly! He's on the brink of a take-over unless I'm very much mistaken.' The rising excitement in his voice came to an abrupt halt as he saw her white face. Then he couldn't resist adding, 'An interview with him will give me just the chance I need to get in with the big boys.'

She turned her back on him, put on the coffee and found a plate. Ordinary everyday things to shut out unwanted thoughts. 'For a journalist, David, you have a very juvenile turn of phrase. You should do well on one of the less attractive tabloids.'

'Thanks.'

'That was not a compliment,' she said sharply.

'No. But I'm working on my thick skin.' There was a little edge to his voice.

'Then keep practising, David. You're obviously going to need it.' She turned to face him, quite unaware of the angry patches of red staining her cheeks. 'I don't know what you want, David, but

I have no influence with Mr Kent. If you want to speak to him I suggest you telephone his office.'

'Have you tried to get past that iron-clad secretary of his?'

'No,' she said tersely.

'No.' His eyes narrowed. 'Of course not. I imagine she has orders to put you straight through.'

'I couldn't say. I've never telephoned him.'

He didn't appear to be convinced.

'Look, Holly, I understand how it is. He's the sort of man that would turn any girl's head.' His voice was cajoling. 'But you're not stupid. You must know that it would be in your own interests to know what he's up to.'

'David!' she protested, her hands so tight on the plate that it was a miracle it didn't break in two. 'I can't make him talk to you.'

'I really think you should try.'

She hid her confusion, her uncertainty in a flurry of activity, checking the bacon, beating the eggs. She had wanted the truth and now it was being offered to her she was refusing to listen in case it confirmed all her worst fears. It was stupid and feeble-minded. She stopped the frantic bustle and sank on to a kitchen stool and faced him.

'You'd better tell me what you've found out.'

'You won't be sorry,' he said, reaching to touch her hand. She withdrew it sharply. He was wrong, she thought; she was sorry already. But, having won his point, he was in no hurry. He ran his hand over his face. 'Look, this'll take some time. Do you mind if I clean up a bit first? I've been driving for hours.'

It was a short reprieve, but, having decided to face whatever had to be endured, she would rather have got it over with as quickly as possible. But she said, 'Up the stairs, first door on the left. Don't take too long, or your breakfast won't be worth eating. And I'm not doing it again.'

She stood over the eggs, stirring them

carefully, all the time aware of the manila envelope lying on the kitchen island behind her.

David had not reappeared by the time they were done, so she dished up and put the plate in the oven to keep warm. Then she wiped her hands and propped herself on one of the kitchen stools, unable to put off the moment any longer. The envelope wasn't sealed and she pulled out the thick wad of paper. Photocopies of news-clips. She glanced at the first one. STAR IN NIGHTCLUB BRAWL.

'I see my sins have found me out.'

Joshua's voice was so close that Holly physically jumped and the newspaper clippings scattered at her feet as she turned to him. So intent had her thoughts been on the man that she might have conjured him up out of the ether. But he didn't look at all ethereal. In dark tailored shorts that revealed a pair of tanned, well-muscled legs and a soft open-necked shirt he looked altogether touchable and, as if to prove it, he bent and kissed her, his lips warm and enticing, sending the blood racing crazily through her veins. He smiled lazily at her. 'Good morning, Holly.'

'You frightened the life out of me, creeping up on me like that,' she scolded, trying to cover her confusion.

'Did I?' He was not in the least contrite. In fact, the creases at the corners of his mouth and eyes deepened if anything. 'Then you shouldn't leave your front door wide open. I did knock, but you were so interested in my past misdemeanours that you obviously didn't hear.' His eyes travelled the length of her throat, apparently fascinated by the deep bare V of skin exposed by her bathrobe.

'Misdemeanours?' She wrapped the bathrobe around her in a self-conscious gesture, tightening the belt, reminded by his warm gaze that she was quite naked beneath it. 'What are you talking about?'

He bent down and picked up the news clippings, raising his eyes to meet hers. The amusement died in them and they blanked. 'Or perhaps I'm mistaken.' He stood up and threw the cuttings down beside her, the change in his voice so marked that her head jerked back in sharp surprise.

'What — ?'

'You've obviously had other things to occupy your mind.'

'Joshua?'

She turned to follow his eyes and saw David in the doorway, his hair wet from the shower, wearing nothing but a thick white towel that he was holding around his waist, and making a brave attempt to hide his dismay as he realised that the one man in the world he was determined to talk to had caught him without his trousers on. He tried a smile. There was no response from the unyielding features of Joshua Kent.

'This is a bit awkward.' David threw a glance at Holly, hoping for rescue. But Holly was unable to help, rigid with shock at what Joshua must be thinking.

'Is it?' Joshua threw into an atmosphere so thick with tension that the words almost bounced off it. 'I'm sure it would help if you put some clothes on.'

'I would, but my bag is in the car.'

Holly made a move to fetch it, but Joshua's hand on her shoulder kept her pinned to her seat. 'Allow me,' he said dangerously. 'Is the boot unlocked?'

'Yes,' David said unhappily. 'I'm parked around the back somewhere. I wasn't sure where I was going.'

'You seem to be doing well enough to me.' He didn't wait for an answer and without even glancing at Holly he turned and strode from the kitchen.

'Well,' David dropped into the silence that followed his departure, 'that's a bit a luck.' He glanced sideways at Holly. 'Now he'll have to talk to me.'

'Eat your breakfast, David, and be quiet.' She banged a plate down in front of him, stuffed the cuttings back in their envelope and left the kitchen, in urgent need of some clothes herself.

When she descended fifteen minutes later, her hair brushed and fastened back from her face by a large tortoiseshell clip, wearing a pair of long cream shorts and a chocolate T-shirt, it was to find Joshua alone in the kitchen pouring himself a cup of coffee. He glanced up at her entrance.

'Where's David?' she asked stiffly as she saw the untouched breakfast.

'Gone to get dressed, I imagine. He suggested that it would be in my best interest to talk to him and then, quite suddenly, remembered that he needed a shave.'

'What have you done to him?' she demanded. 'He'd only just arrived, for heaven's sake.'

'I know. His engine was still warm.'

'Still . . . So!' she exploded. 'That's why you were so keen to fetch his bag. To check whether he had been here all night. Did you actually think that I would . . . after . . . ?' She couldn't even say it, she was so angry.

He leaned back against the sink, his face impassive. 'If he'd turned up last night, just after I'd gone, I think he would have tried to take advantage of the situation. Or maybe you're going to tell me that he wouldn't do anything so underhand?'

'Then you shouldn't have gone,' she snapped and her face flamed. 'I didn't ask him to come, Joshua.' She had to warn him. 'It's you he's after. Apparently he's found out about Ashbrooke . . .'

'So he said. He wants an interview on the subject of my take-over of Ashbrooke Leisure.'

She was very still. So it was true. As the reality of what it meant struck home, she thought she might be sick. 'He said you're taking them over. Is he right?'

'Everything was signed yesterday afternoon. Luigi is now the proud owner of the Hall and I have a new company. So I'm afraid that if that's his scoop David has come galloping after cold news.'

'But . . . are you . . . do you . . . intend to develop Highfield?'

'Would it matter?' he asked, and the importance of her answer was all too evident in the intensity of his expression.

She took a deep breath. 'Yes, Joshua. I'm rather afraid it would. If you've bought the company on the expectation of profits from Highfield, I'm afraid you've made a mistake. I won't sell. You should have let me sign the contract in France when I didn't care, instead of making me come home to do it.'

'If I'd had the slightest intention of allowing you to sell Highfield, my dear Holly, I would have done just that.'

'If . . . Oh, Joshua,' she said. 'What have you done?'

'Done, my dear? I've sold a house I had no use for and bought a business that I intend to expand. One deal to finance another. One way or another I expect to make a great deal of money.'

A movement in the doorway alerted them to the fact that they were no longer alone.

'Can I quote you on that, Mr Kent?' David Grantham enquired brazenly as he sauntered into the kitchen.

'David!' Holly warned, fierce as any vixen defending her cubs, and Joshua glanced at her in surprise before turning his full attention on the man on the other side of the room.

His expression hardened. 'Quote me at your peril, Mr Grantham.'

David barely flinched despite the lash in the other man's voice. 'Or what?' he demanded recklessly. 'You're not fireproof, Mr Kent; I already have a national newspaper ready to back me with this story and I've seen enough this morning to know I *have* got a story. Now I'm simply giving you an opportunity to make a statement before I go to press.'

'I can't think what information you might have that would excite such interest.' The chill factor in Joshua's voice dipped to sub-zero. 'Perhaps you would care to enlighten me.'

David's voice rose in triumph. 'An executor taking advantage of a vulnerable young woman who has just inherited a valuable estate is bad enough, Mr

Kent. But when he's clearly seduced her to achieve his ends . . . ' He glanced from one face, white with shock, to the glacial features of Joshua Kent. 'I think you take my point?' He sat down at the breakfast-bar, produced a small tape recorder from his pocket and switched it on. 'Now. What would you like to say to my readers?'

9

For a moment nothing happened. Then David was hanging from Joshua's fist by his shirt-front.

'I think, Grantham,' he said, with paralysing insistence, 'you'd better go. Or it's quite possible that you will be the subject of your own front page.'

'Joshua . . . ' Holly made a move towards him, but he stopped her with a glance.

'Stay out of this Holly.'

'I think it's a little late for that,' she said, and with a little lift of her chin she went on quickly, before she could think twice, 'and in this case I'm quite capable of defending my own reputation.'

He brushed this aside and continued to glare at David with extreme prejudice. 'You don't have to. We both know that. But this creature won't care who gets hurt so long as he has a story that will sell newspapers.' He gave David a little shake. 'Will you, Mr Grantham? Tell the lady the truth.' David opened his mouth, but never had an opportunity to tell Holly anything.

'The truth, Joshua . . . ' she declared, interrupting with biting resolution, her tiger's eyes sparkling with fury that either of them should feel entitled to exclude her from something that involved her so personally. 'The truth is that if he prints one word of that story I will sue him and his newspaper until they retract in headlines a foot high.' She took a deep breath as both men turned to her in astonishment. But she hadn't finished. 'I don't know what you've done, Joshua. Frankly, it no longer matters, since I have no intention of selling Highfield to you or anyone else. But I will not have anyone believing I'm so pathetically weak-willed that I could be *seduced* out of anything.'

Joshua frowned and let David down

rather suddenly, having apparently forgotten him in his concern for her. 'No, Holly.' He took her by the shoulders, gripping her painfully, a fierce protectiveness in his face. 'They'll destroy you if you take them on. Tear you to shreds.'

'Let them try. If necessary I'll prove them liars.' She lifted her chin, two bright spots of pink staining her cheeks. 'I can do that, I assure you.'

'Prove?' For a moment he stared at her in disbelief. Then he swore softly.

David cleared his throat. 'I think I'd better go.'

Joshua glanced at him, then at the plate of cold scrambled egg and congealing bacon. 'Sit down, Grantham, and eat your breakfast; you're not going anywhere until I've talked to you.' It was not an invitation that could be refused and David sank unhappily back on to the stool. Then Joshua turned to Holly and took her arm quite firmly, his mouth compressed into a hard, straight line. 'Holly? I could do with some fresh air.'

He opened the kitchen door and they walked out into the garden and out along the clifftop where the breeze was blowing, fresh and cool from the sea.

'What will you do to him?' Holly asked, tentative in the face of such implacable fury.

He glanced at her and relaxed sufficiently for his lip to curve into a cynical smile. 'I ought to throw him off the cliff.'

Encouraged, she said, 'If you do that I'll have to find another lodger. Whatever else David might be, he pays the rent on time.'

'Sell the damned house and then you wouldn't have to worry about it.' At her stricken expression he stiffened. 'Oh, don't fret. I won't damage the man. In fact I'll give him an interview. That should be enough to make his career, even without the prurient side-interest of my sex life.'

'You don't have to go that far. I'm very angry with him.'

'Are you? Why? You asked him to

check up on me.'

'No, Joshua. I didn't. I telephoned him to let him know I was home, that was all. He's jealous, I can see that, although heaven knows why. I've never given him the slightest encouragement. In fact he used to regularly bring his girlfriends home for the night.'

'And recently?'

'Well, he's stayed in a lot more . . . oh, I see. I didn't realise. A bit slow-witted of me.'

'Perhaps, but if he's that keen on you, what's he playing at?'

'He clearly thinks you're trying to cheat me in some way. And I'm afraid that is my fault. I mentioned Ashbrooke Leisure wanted to buy the house and he had found out you were taking them over. Put the two together and it reeks of something a bit nasty in the woodshed.'

'Do you think I would cheat you, Holly?'

'I think,' she said carefully, 'that you'd better explain exactly what's been going on. Is there a buyer for Highfield or not?'

'If you want to sell, then I'll cover the sum I told you was on offer. But I was rather hoping that the prospect of losing the place would make you think twice.'

'Then you were right.' She offered a tentative smile. 'You always are, apparently. So what are you going to do about David?'

'I find it incredible that he would have hurt you to get at me. It's hard to forgive, Holly.'

'Is it? Don't you feel just a little bit sorry for him?' she asked him.

His eyes softened as he looked at her. 'Possibly,' he conceded. 'But I hope to heaven that he never finds out.' He thought for a moment. 'He'll have to forget the tabloids. But I'll give him a piece that any one of the quality papers will fall over themselves for. That way he might be persuaded to forget that he saw me making love to you in your kitchen at six o'clock in the morning.'

'But you'd only just walked in,' she protested. 'You were dressed.'

'You weren't.'

'Oh!' Her face was a picture of confusion. 'You shouldn't have noticed.'

'I'm only human.'

'Not that human,' she retorted quickly, then put up her hands to cover hot cheeks.

He laughed softly. 'Don't you think that in the circumstances it's probably just as well I didn't accept your invitation to stay last night?' He took her hands away from her face and regarded her with grave eyes. 'There would have been precious little left to prove my innocence with.' After an almost imperceptible pause he said, 'Unless of course you were bluffing?'

She made an effort at a lack of concern that she was very far from feeling. 'You'll have to call me to find out, won't you? Are you innocent, Joshua?'

He shook his head, a slow smile lighting his eyes. 'Don't ever play poker,

Holly. You haven't got the face for it.' Then he said, 'You obviously didn't get very far with Grantham's press cuttings.'

Grateful that he had let her off the hook, she sighed with relief. 'I haven't read any of them.' Then she glanced at him sideways. 'What have you done that's so bad?'

'Read all the news that's fit to print and I'll leave you to make up your own mind. But when you do, bear in mind what he would have made of that scene in the kitchen and take it all with just a pinch of salt.'

She turned and looked at him, her lips parted in soft laughter. 'Joshua Kent, are you telling me that you have a *reputation*?'

His grip on her elbow tightened momentarily. They had been gradually walking back towards the house and he indicated the garden seat and sat down beside her. She found her breath quite suddenly caught in her throat, wondering what on earth he could be going to tell her with such a solemn face. What could be that bad? He propped one elbow on the back of the seat and began to toy with a wayward strand of her hair, wrapping it tightly around his finger, holding her captive by that slender thread as surely as if he had her in chains.

'Once, Holly, when you were still in pigtails, I made a complete ass of myself over an actress. I was young enough, and I have to say green enough, when I made my first really big deal to attract the notice of the Press. Idiot that I was, I actually thought that it made me someone important. So important that it was easy to believe that Shelly had fallen in love with me. What she actually loved was publicity. She was very beautiful, very exotic. At least five years older than me.' He paused, a sudden glint in his eye. 'Possibly more.' Then he shrugged, as if it didn't matter. 'I was quite bowled over. But youthful pride is fierce and when I overheard a remark at a party about her 'cradle-snatching', well — ' he shrugged

' — I'm afraid I behaved very badly. I won't draw a picture, but I was lucky not to be charged with assault. The ensuing publicity caused me a great deal of embarrassment and everyone else much amusement, except for the lady involved. The affair ended somewhat abruptly.' He smiled slightly. 'The incident taught me a lot. Mainly about self-control. But for a long time I was pursued in the hope that I might make the same mistake again. And they have a long memory in Fleet Street; they never miss an opportunity to remind their readers what you did in the past, if given the slightest excuse.'

'Oh.' She hid a smile.

'Quite. Ridiculous. And I've never come so close to hitting anyone again as I did this morning and that would have been a very big mistake. An exclusive interview will be quite a coup for a young reporter trying to break into the big time. And it's a small price to pay for a little discretion.'

'But he wouldn't . . . '

'Wouldn't he? He's ambitious, Holly. He would like you to be in love with him, but you're not and he knows it. Would you trust him with the story of your life?' Put baldly, like that, Holly had to concede that she wouldn't. She hadn't. She shook her head.

But with that knowledge came something else: a clarity of mind that had been eluding her all the long, dark hours of the night. Because with the discovery that she didn't trust David came the equally startling knowledge that she would trust Joshua not only with the story of her life, but life itself.

She turned to him and the twirling of his finger immediately stopped as her face was suddenly inches from his. It was an effort to concentrate under the perilous nearness of a pair of eyes so clear and deep that she thought it would be possible to drown in them. She turned quickly away.

'Thank you for helping me to see that I should stay, Joshua.'

'I actually quite enjoyed myself.'

'Not as much as you might have.'

'I didn't want to confuse anything.'

'No? Then you'd better ring Marcus and explain what you've been doing. I think he must be very confused.'

'Marcus was rather upset when he phoned me yesterday afternoon. Demanded that I tell you the truth or he would do the decent thing. I had a devil of a job with him.'

'I began to suspect that something was wrong after I'd had lunch with him. He tried very hard, but clearly was paddling way out of his depth.'

'You're very quick, Holly.'

'Not quick enough. Why didn't you just suggest I stay put for a while?'

'This from a girl who prefers her advice upside-down?' His voice, his eyes, his whole body challenged her to admit the truth. 'You had to make your own decision. Stay here because it was what you wanted more than anything else in the whole world. But you made it damned difficult. I thought if I could just get you home I could work something out. But I never expected so many questions.'

'Why on earth did you say Ashbrooke Leisure wanted to buy the house?'

'It was the first name that came into my head. I could hardly use one of my own companies.'

'And the caravans?'

'Mary's father tried to get a scheme through years ago. He thought that because he was mayor he could do what he liked. He found out differently. I thought it was suitably gruesome and, because of that, perfectly likely.'

'You went to a lot of trouble.' She stood up, pulling away from him, unable to think with the warm heat of his body against her, needing to put a space between them, needing to look away from those disquieting eyes. 'Why didn't you stay last night?' she asked a little stiffly.

There was a moment of utter silence. 'I didn't want your decision to be influenced by any other factors, Holly. You've been through a difficult time. I didn't want you to do anything you might regret later.' He rose quickly to his feet. 'You are sure?' She waited, breathless, uncertain what he meant. 'About staying?'

For a moment she stared at the dark, tanned V of his chest where his shirt revealed a few dark hairs, forcing herself to face the fact that he had simply been keeping a promise to a dying woman. His kiss had been a response to the desperate need he had seen in her eyes, to their closeness on the back of that crazy motorbike, to the tension caused by continual bickering. A thousand reasons, but none of them important.

Now he had fulfilled his promise, done everything her mother had asked of him, and he could walk away and get on with the rest of his life with a clear conscience. She must do the same.

'Yes, Joshua,' she said. 'I'm quite sure about staying.' She shrugged quickly free of his touch, stepped around him and walked quickly down the path. 'I found something yesterday that made up my mind for me,' she said with a forced cheerfulness, coming to a halt in front of the hidden studio, then faltered. 'Oh, I haven't brought the keys.'

'You've found the studio?'

She turned on him. 'You knew it was here and you didn't tell me?' She felt stupidly close to tears and that wouldn't do, so she put her hands on her hips and her head on one side and demanded, 'What else haven't you told me, Joshua Kent?'

He raised his hand to her chin, tilting it up to read the expression in her face. 'One or two things, Holly Carpenter, but there's no rush, if you're staying.' He glanced at the studio. 'And I knew you'd find this place sooner or later. It's been here a long time, just waiting for you.'

'Waiting?' She thought of the pristine tubes of paint, the new brushes, the fresh canvases. She knew something had been missing and it had been the smell of paint and turpentine. The studio had never been used. 'Mary did that for me?' He nodded and let his hand fall to his side. It was easier to think without his warm hand under her chin, yet a little lonely, and she shivered slightly. 'You never said a word.'

'On the contrary, I think perhaps I said rather too many. I thought you were a cold, uncaring young woman who had quite deliberately chosen to ignore her natural mother. I did everything Mary asked of me, to the letter, but frankly I hoped you would just go away and never set foot in Highfield, or Ashbrooke, again.'

'So why did you make me come back?'

'Because I made a mistake.' His eyes were shadowed in the cool shade of the studio. Unreadable. 'I confess that from the moment I met you I had my doubts, but I refused to listen to them. The facts spoke for themselves. It was quite clear that you were simply coming with me because you thought that you might miss out on a valuable inheritance if you didn't.'

'That wasn't why I came.'

'No. That caricature was quite a shock, though. Did I really make that bad an impression?'

'Yes,' she admitted, embarrassed. 'But you've changed. I couldn't draw that now.' Then, realising that this betrayed her own change of heart, she turned from him and looked at the house, bathed in sunshine. 'But there was no need to come and fetch me. I would have come back.'

'I couldn't be sure. And I wanted you here.' Before she could work out exactly what he meant by that, he had his arm around her shoulder and was leading her back to the house. 'Come on; I've been putting off the evil moment, but I think I'd better get this interview over with, then I can throw Grantham out with an easy conscience.'

'I can manage that myself, Joshua. But it's a long drive and it is the weekend. He really ought to stay until tomorrow.'

'He should have thought of that

before he came bothering you. If he's too tired to go home he'll have to stay in a hotel.'

★ ★ ★

David's face, as he followed Joshua back into the sitting-room a couple of hours later, was an odd mixture of elation and dejection. Clearly he had got most of what he wanted, but at a cost.

'If you telephone my secretary on Monday she'll make an appointment for your photographer to come to my office,' Joshua said, then added, in case it wasn't absolutely clear, 'I don't want to see you again.'

Joshua returned to the study, leaving David to say goodbye to Holly and tender his apologies, which he did with less grace than she might have expected in the circumstances.

'I wouldn't have said anything about the two of you,' he said finally, unable to contain his resentment any longer.

'He didn't have to threaten me.'

He looked so much like a small boy that Holly felt quite sorry for him. She had no idea what Joshua's idea of a threat was, but could well imagine that it wouldn't be much fun to be on the receiving end of it.

'There's nothing to tell, David.'

'No? That was two other people I saw kissing this morning, was it?'

'David,' she warned. 'You have more than you could possibly have hoped for. Leave it at that.'

'I know. I should be grateful. It was just that . . . Oh, what's the use? Who could compete with someone like Joshua Kent?' He made an angry gesture in the direction of the study. 'He's got everything. Including you, apparently.'

Wrong again, David, she thought. He hasn't got me, because he doesn't want me. But she had no intention of giving him any hope. 'Once you've a grand job in London you'll find someone special and forget all about me,' she assured him, trying hard not to be too impatient.

He looked at her pityingly. 'I might find someone else, Holly. But I'll never forget you.' He paused in the doorway. 'Just don't let him hurt you.' Too late, she thought. Far too late for that.

'Has he gone?' Joshua looked up from the tape recorder as Holly searched him out in the study a little later.

'Yes. What are you doing?'

He pocketed the cassette. 'Just a few precautions, in case he decides to forget our agreement.' He pulled a face. 'What a miserable start to a warm and sunny Saturday. I came to take you sailing and now it's the middle of the morning.'

'Sailing? I've never been sailing.'

'Well, now is a very good time to learn. Ashbrooke Leisure is about to launch a new class of yacht. The prototype awaits your pleasure.'

She had thought, in that moment when she had turned at the sound of his voice and he had kissed her, that he had changed his mind. Come back to finish what they had barely begun. But no. He had made her come back to Ashbrooke and now felt it his duty to look after her. She had no wish to be a duty.

'It sounds lovely, but please don't feel you have to entertain me, Joshua. I'm sure there are dozens of other things you could be doing.'

'Hundreds,' he assured her, with a perfectly straight face. 'We could drive up to Dartmoor if you'd prefer?'

'It's all right, Joshua,' she said, determined to let him see that she wasn't going to make a fuss just because he had kissed her until her bones melted. He had probably kissed dozens of girls just like that. He couldn't possibly have known that for her it was a totally new experience. 'You've done everything you had to do. I'll always be very grateful.' She put out her hand very firmly, a gesture that gave them both a graceful exit. He took it in his own, larger, darker one and held it quite gently.

'Are you telling me to go?' he asked in a smooth drawl that immediately threatened to overturn her resolve. His grip tightened imperceptibly as she tried to withdraw her hand from his.

'I . . . I think it would be best.'

'For whom?'

'For — '

But apparently he didn't need an answer. He provided his own. 'If you're saying it would be best for me, Holly, I have to tell you that that's an impudent presumption on your part.' She opened her mouth to deny it, but he continued, 'But if you're trying to tell me that it would be best for you . . . ' This time the pause was endless, but she had nothing to say ' . . . then I intend to prove you wrong.' He jerked her in one swift movement into his arms and pinned her against him, his hands at her waist, her bare legs pressed against the hard, hairy length of his thighs.

'Joshua!' she protested. 'Let me go!' And she pushed furiously against his chest.

'Of course,' he went on, as if nothing out of the ordinary were happening. As if her heart were not rushing headlong to obliteration. As if her body were still all her own and not simply a quivering extension of his. 'You could simply admit your mistake. Say, I'm sorry, Joshua. I'd love to spend the day with you. Try it.'

'No — ' One hand remained at her waist, effortlessly containing her attempts to free herself. The other began to move in a slow, kindling caress upwards along her spine and for a moment she was paralysed by the slow spread of fire that seeped through her veins. Then she gasped and began to struggle against him in earnest. His full lower lip curved in a sensuous smile and his eyes darkened and quite suddenly she realised that she was not helping herself. Not one bit. She stopped abruptly, her breath coming in short ragged gasps as she fought to overcome her own desire.

'Well?' He waited a moment, holding her against the warm, still length of his body, driving her almost beyond the limit of her self-control. Then his mouth began to dip towards hers.

'I'm sorry, Joshua,' she rasped out urgently. 'I'd love to spend the day with you.' His mouth paused, inches from her own, but he didn't loosen his grip an iota.

'Sure?' he said. 'I'm perfectly willing to demonstrate.' Neither of them was oblivious to the quiver that shot through her.

'Yes, Joshua.' She could hardly speak, but his look demanded more. 'I'd love to spend the day with you.' She forced the words out in a series of hoarse, panting breaths.

'That's better.' She almost collapsed with relief as he loosened his grip. Then he said, 'Oh, what the hell?' And he kissed her anyway.

10

Holly's lips parted on an urgent protest and that was her first mistake. What might have been almost nothing, the merest tease of a kiss, became altogether different as, with a groan something like agony, he pulled her fiercely into his arms, his tongue stroking swiftly along hers to begin the sweetest exploration of her mouth. His touch turned her bones to liquid fire and she melted against him, no longer able to offer any resistance to the man taking control of her senses and making them his slave. Even her hands, which had been pressing against his chest, fighting uselessly against his domination of her will, slid traitorously upwards to wind themselves around his neck, leaving her quite defenceless. And that was her second mistake.

His hands swiftly loosened the T-shirt from her waistband and then slipped under the cloth where the sensitive pads of his fingers began to work a deeper kind of magic, sending warm, electric tremors flickering across the silky smooth skin of her back. He reached the fastening of her bra, disposed of it and then his hands moved swiftly to cup the firm ripeness of her breasts and torment the burgeoning tips of her nipples under his thumbs.

Holly made a small sound, somewhere between a purr and a moan, and pressed her hips wantonly against Joshua as she felt the urgent stirring of his passion.

He drew back with a sharp exclamation and searched her face, his eyes dark and heavy-lidded with arousal. 'If you want me to go, Holly,' he warned, the grating texture of his voice a further torment, 'you had better stop doing that right now.'

She smiled lazily back at him, her cheeks flushed, her large amber eyes almost black. 'Do you still want to spend the day on Dartmoor?' she challenged, her voice low and husky. And that was her third mistake.

Joshua Kent said something quite rude on the subject of Dartmoor. Then he bent and caught her behind the knees, swinging her up into his arms to carry her swiftly up the stairs.

She knew she should protest. She should make some show of resistance. But she didn't want to. She was beyond caring what might happen afterwards; she only knew that she wanted this man. This arrogant, unbearable, dominating man, who had appeared uninvited upon her doorstep and turned her life upside-down.

He shouldered open the bedroom door and then placed her very gently on the bed. For a moment, he held her there, caged by hands on either side of her body, barely touching her, but even a foot apart the heat of his body was searing her to a flaming desire that only he could quench.

Then he lifted one hand and trailed his fingers across her burning lips.

'You're beautiful, Holly.'

'If I am, Joshua, it's because you've made me feel beautiful.'

His mouth touched her lips so briefly that she felt instantly bereft, then her complaint became a sigh as it began a slow and sensuous exploration of the delicate skin under her chin, along the curve of her throat, trailing the firebrand of his tongue down to the edge of her T-shirt.

'Don't stop,' she moaned and moved to throw it off. Get rid of all her clothes. But he caught her hand.

'I'll undress you in my own good time.'

She lay back against the pillows, her platinum hair spread like a wild halo. 'Don't take too long.' The words shocked her. Never had she been like this. She had been teased for her reserve, sworn at on one unpleasant occasion before she had learned to quell expectations before they got out of hand. But love had woken some new, wilder side to her nature.

For a moment Joshua was very still. Holding back with some last vestige of self-control. 'Holly,' he said, his voice ragged with the effort, 'if you have any doubts, say now. If I take you, I keep you. Forever.'

She opened her eyes fully and looked at him, the clamped-down jaw as he waited for her to be certain, the grey eyes shimmering with passion. Doubts? What doubts could there be? Even on that first day when they had glared at one another across the shabby sitting-room at home she had known they were fencing on a razor-edge. He had jarred against her, stirring the slumbering passion that was now thundering through her veins, setting up a raw, sexual tension, and deep inside she had recognised the danger. Now, when she had fallen helplessly, hopelessly in love with the man there could be no doubts. No matter what happened afterwards, she wanted this moment. And he was right; she would hold it in her heart forever.

She laughed softly, catching at the hem of his shirt and easing it up his back, her fingers doing a little teasing on her own account as they strayed across his chest and down the flat, hard stomach. Her lips parted in delight as he drew in a sharp breath, rejoicing that she had the power to render him momentarily speechless. 'Does that answer your question, Joshua? Now, how much longer are you going to keep a lady waiting?' She flipped open the button of his shorts.

'Dear God,' he murmured. 'Don't . . .' But what she musn't do was never voiced as the doorbell rang, shattering the bubble of the private world into which they had retreated. They both froze.

'Would David come back?' Joshua asked her after the first stunned silence. Holly shook her head, the crazy enchantment already evaporating with the loud intrusion of the outside world. Joshua began to roll from the bed, already tucking the soft polo shirt back into his shorts.

'Ignore it,' she pleaded, catching at his hands. 'Whoever it is will go away.'

'With my car parked on the front doorstep?' He shook his head. 'At least David had the sense to drive round the back.'

'We could be on the beach. Anywhere.'

But the point became academic as they heard the sound of the door opening and a voice calling out, 'Is anyone home?'

'Oh, God.' He stepped back and drew a deep breath, running his hands through his hair in an effort to tidy it. 'It's Mrs Austin. She worked for Mary and she's been coming in a couple of days a week while the house has been empty. I phoned her yesterday and said she should come and see you. I might have known she wouldn't wait until Monday. She's a terrible old gossip, Holly, and she'll expect every detail of your life history before she leaves.'

'I haven't got a life history,' Holly said scratchily. And at this rate she never would have. She got unsteadily to her feet and caught sight of herself in the mirror. She winced. 'Joshua, I can't. Look at me.'

For a moment he did just that. Then he wrenched himself back into the real world and whisked her silently into the bathroom. He wrung out a cold flannel and held it to her cheeks.

'Hello? Miss Carpenter?' Joshua's eyes warned her to be silent and they stayed perfectly still while the footsteps began to climb the stairs. Then the steps stopped and retreated and after a moment they heard her on the path outside.

'She's gone into the garden to look for us.' He held her for a moment, steadying her, handing her a hairbrush. 'Just think of something else, Holly. Something nasty.' He groaned softly and pushed her away. 'Go. You'll be fine. Make her a cup of tea. I'll be down in a moment to rescue you.' He caught her by the shoulders and dropped a brief kiss on her mouth. 'Don't worry.

She doesn't bite. She only looks as if she might.'

Her legs were a little wobbly as she made her way back down the stairs, still certain that the world and its wife would know exactly what she had been doing on this sunny Saturday morning.

'Hello?' she called. 'Mrs Austin?'

Holly moved quickly towards the woman coming in through the garden door, looking about her uncertainly. They had met briefly at Mary's funeral, but Holly had been wearing a prim suit with a black velvet hat covering her hair. Now Mrs Austin audibly drew breath.

'Miss Carpenter.' She couldn't take her eyes off Holly.

'Won't you come in? Mr Kent told me you would probably call today.'

'Well, dear, I hope it isn't inconvenient, but I thought I'd better come and see what hours you wanted. If you want me to work for you at all, that is.' She looked up the stairs and Holly could almost hear the wheels of her mind working. 'Is that Mr Joshua's car outside?'

'Yes, he's . . . ' Holly forced a smile. 'Would you like some tea, Mrs Austin? A sandwich perhaps? It must be very near lunchtime.' She glanced at her watch. It was not quite ten-thirty.

Mrs Austin looked at her a little oddly. 'A cup of tea would be very nice. But nothing to eat. I can't stay long.' She threw a glance back over her shoulder at the stairs as she allowed herself to be shepherded into the sitting-room.

Holly took another deep, steadying breath as she filled the kettle, wondering what on earth Joshua was up to. Surely he didn't intend to hide upstairs? That would really give the woman something to think about. Perhaps he expected her to make some excuse. She tried to clear the cotton wool from her mind and think of something. A blocked sink, perhaps? No, Mrs Austin looked the sort of woman to roll up her sleeves and go and deal with that sort of problem herself, given half a chance.

With hands still shaking, she laid a tray with three of the best cups, filled the delicate milk jug and put out the sugar basin. She poured the boiling water into the teapot and then found some chocolate biscuits. There was still no sign of Joshua when she carried it into the sitting-room and set it down on the low table before the sofa.

'Well, here we are,' she said, smiling with a confidence she was far from feeling, and covered the ensuing moments with a flurry of polite queries regarding milk and sugar, holding off the question she sensed Mrs Austin was dying to ask.

Finally there was nothing more to do and she raised her cup to her lips just as Mrs Austin began, 'Is Mr Joshua going to join us — ?'

'Mrs Austin! How good of you to come.' Holly's cup rattled in her saucer as she raised her eyes and saw Joshua, dark hair dusted with cobwebs, his arms full of photograph albums. 'I

271

promised Miss Carpenter I would go up into the loft for her this morning,' he said confidentially, sinking down beside the older woman on the sofa. 'I knew there must be a lot of old photographs somewhere and she's a bit like Mary: scared of spiders.' His eyes glinted softly at Holly as he took the cup she offered. 'Isn't that right?'

'I'm afraid so. Witless.'

Mrs Austin tutted. 'If you want anything down from the loft, Miss Carpenter, you just ask me. No need to go bothering a busy man like Mr Joshua.'

'Please call me Holly.'

'Holly. What a pretty name. Of course, you were a Christmas baby.'

'Christmas Eve,' Holly confirmed.

Joshua drank his tea and stood up. 'I'd better go and leave you two to sort out your business. Unless I can do anything else for you, Holly?' His brazen look from behind Mrs Austin's back was blush-making, but Holly managed somehow to keep a straight face.

'Not right now, Joshua. But could

you drop by this evening? I have one or two things you really ought to see,' she said, and placed her cup on the tray without a sound. 'If you can spare the time, that is? Mrs Austin tells me that you are a very busy man. I'd hate to take advantage of your . . . ' she paused and managed a slow smile. ' . . . good nature.'

It was his turn to struggle. 'I think I can manage that. About seven?'

'Perhaps I can offer you dinner. A small thank-you for all your kindness.'

'Well, that's very thoughtful,' he said quite briskly. 'But there'll be quite a lot to get through. Better leave dinner until later.'

'Shall I show you out?'

'I know the way.' He mouthed a silent kiss from the doorway and retreated before her detached manner disintegrated entirely.

Mrs Austin had settled herself on the sofa and made herself at home. 'It's a while since I saw these old albums.' She produced a cloth from her pocket and wiped the dust off the top one and opened it. 'Well, now. Look at that. It's Mr and Mrs Graham and Miss Mary when she couldn't have been more than ten years old.'

Holly joined the woman on the sofa. Her grandfather had a stern expression, his wife looked serene and Mary . . . well, Mary looked exactly as she had at the same age. A little bit too thin, her fair hair bleached white by the sun.

They turned the pages; Mrs Austin knew all the people, chattered on, full of gossip. There was even one of her mother as a young girl, staying with her cousin.

There was another picture of her grandfather looking very important in a red robe and chain of office. 'That was the year Miss Mary's father was mayor,' Mrs Austin explained, having taken it upon herself to explain the entire family history.

'What was he like?'

Mrs Austin hesitated. 'A bit stiff.

Miss Mary found it hard, I think, especially after her mother left.'

'Left?'

The other woman's eyes gleamed briefly with the excitement of a new audience for old news. 'She left him for another man. Caused a high old scandal and Miss Mary was kept on a pretty tight rein by her father afterwards, I can tell you.' She shook her head. 'A mistake, that. Even when she insisted she must go and look after your poor mother when she was expecting you. He made such a fuss, I thought that the heaven would fall in. But he could see how set she was and I think she would have gone anyway. She was always fond of your mother.' She sighed. 'I thought that when he died it would be different, but she must have been thirty by then and I suppose she'd got into the habit of being alone. Not that she was ever lonely, of course. She was always busy.'

'You've worked for the family a long time?'

'Mrs Graham took me on when she was first married. I'd just left school. Just a slip of a thing. Then they took on Austin for the garden and to drive and me and him hit it off. We lived in the cottage then. Miss Mary left it to me, you know.'

'Yes, I know.'

Mrs Austin turned another page. 'Oh, look, it's Mr Joshua's father. He and Mr Graham were both magistrates.' She looked up from the picture. 'You and Miss Mary could have been twins if you'd been the same age.'

It was the sort of photograph taken by the hundred at major functions. It was a dinner. Mr Graham was clearly making an effort to look happy. Mr Kent, perhaps twenty years younger than she had seen him in France a few days before, his hair thicker, slightly darker, looked totally at ease, smiling across at Mary. And Mrs Austin had been right. The likeness was too striking to miss. She touched her hair. Maybe she ought to darken it a little.

'Were the two families friendly?' she asked, to redirect Mrs Austin's attention.

'I don't know about friends.' She shrugged. 'In the last couple of years Mr Joshua has been a great help to your cousin, but I don't think Mr Alexander Kent ever was much of a friend to Mr Graham. They were very different sorts of men. He came to the house, of course. They had town business.'

'Alexander? Is that his name?' Her voice sounded the same. But nothing would ever be quite the same again. She laid the tip of her finger on the photograph of Joshua's father and remembered a half-imagined tear as he had turned away from her. Had he suspected?

'Yes. He's living in France now. A very good-looking man, like Mr Joshua.' She nodded in the direction of the door and raised a knowing eyebrow. 'Mrs Kent was a very forbearing lady.'

'Alexander?' she repeated.

'Yes, dear.'

'You're sure?' Mrs Austin glanced at

her a little oddly and Holly let it go. Of course she was sure. The woman went on and on, turning the pages of the album, chattering on, full of small-town gossip, but Holly had stopped listening. She responded automatically when there was a gap in the monologue that seemed to demand it, but she had no idea what was actually being said.

Eventually Holly's silence must have seeped through. 'Well, I mustn't stay here taking up all your day. I'll see you on Monday, Miss Carpenter.'

'What?'

'Monday. I've got a key. If you're not here I'll just get on.' There was a seemingly endless list of instructions about what to do with laundry and shopping lists but finally she left and Holly found herself standing on the back doorstep watching the woman wobble down the drive on her bicycle.

After a while she made herself close the door. Her limbs still worked, but there was a numbness in her head. Not even a pain. Nothing. She knew she should be grateful. As she climbed up the stairs, each step a mountain to be overcome by sheer will-power, she knew without doubt that the pain would come.

She opened the bedside drawer, where the Chinese notebook lay. She knew the words by heart. Read it constantly to comfort herself that Mary had borne her out of a deep and lasting love. It had been no quick fumble, regretted and furtively dealt with. Now the comfort turned to ash in her heart.

She picked up the book, but she had no need to open the cover to read that first damning sentence. 'A came to the house today and made me a woman.'

She had scarcely wondered who the mysterious 'A' might be, too wrapped up in her concerns about Mary. It had been stupid. She had had a father as well as a mother, but she had thought that the unknown man did not matter. Was unimportant. She opened the book. But there was no mistake.

A came to the house today and made me a woman. I knew he would come. After that kiss, that glorious, wonderful kiss, I knew he had to come. But he was so clever, so cool! 'Is your father at home?' he asked, nothing in his eyes to show that he knew father was at a committee meeting that was going to last forever. He went on endlessly about it last night at the dinner, until I thought he would drive us all mad with boredom. Now I can only hope that he will always announce his plans with such glorious forethought.

The bed was rumpled where their bodies had lain an hour before. Had it looked like that when Mary had lain with Alexander Kent? Holly wondered, and a cold, clammy hand clutched at her heart as she realised the horror of what had so nearly happened. She straightened the quilt with shaking fingers, obliterating the evidence. But that didn't help and in a second she was tearing at the bedclothes, taking off the sheets, the cover, the pillowcase and pushing them out of sight into the bathroom. Then she stood for a moment, her chest hurting with the effort of breathing, and in the silence she thought she could hear the sound of her heart breaking.

It was a while before she could think straight. She found some linen in the airing cupboard and remade the bed. Packed her bag. Tidied everything carefully so that no one would ever know she had been at Highfield. Then, when she had rehearsed what she would say, she went to the telephone to call Joshua. The phone rang twice and then was picked up.

'Joshua — ' She started to speak, then realised with a sickening jolt that there was no one there.

'This is Joshua Kent,' the recording announced. 'I'm not available at the moment, but leave your name and number and I'll get back to you.'

There was a short tone and then the

tape began to run. A sob caught her voice and she put the phone down quickly. It was a long time before she could speak again and she didn't try the telephone.

If she phoned and cancelled their dinner arrangement he would simply come around and find out what was wrong. Even if she could put him off for this evening, there was no guarantee that he wouldn't come after her.

She would have to convince him, face to face, that she had changed her mind. It wouldn't be easy. It would be the hardest thing she had ever done. But it was the only way. She would die rather than tell him the truth, not after this morning, when she had encouraged him so wantonly that her body now burned for shame. He must never know that he was her half-brother.

★ ★ ★

He arrived at seven, prompt to the minute, and when, white-faced under the extra blusher she had applied to give herself some colour, Holly opened the door, he stood for a moment and took in the pale beauty standing before him. She had made herself dress up. Wear the soft black chiffon dress that she loved. She wanted him to see her at her best. And she had made herself up for him. When she had finished, he might hate her, but this way he would never suspect her misery.

He was holding a single red rose and after a moment he offered it to her. She took it, her fingers trembling so much that the leaves quivered like aspen.

He put down a bottle of champagne on the hall table and held her hands between his. 'Am I causing that?' he asked.

'You?' Her voice came out as a squeak. 'Good gracious, no. I think I'm getting a cold.' And she shivered convulsively in apparent confirmation.

His forehead creased in the slightest frown. 'Did you get so cold last night?'

'I . . . I suppose I must have.'

He had dressed for the occasion, gloriously formal in a dinner-jacket, the black broadcloth moulded to his shoulders in perfection, the white shirt-front plain, as she would have expected.

'Well, champagne is the perfect cure. Shall we open it now?' He led the way to the dining-room and bent to extract two glasses from the cupboard.

'How wonderful!' She swallowed hard, then put on the brightest smile she could, before he straightened and saw the betraying misery in her eyes. 'I've had some wonderful news, so a celebration is quite in order.'

'Oh?' He discarded the foil and glanced up at her, catching the oddness in her manner. 'And what is that? Sold a painting?'

The pulse in her temple was hammering quite dreadfully and she put up her fingers to try to steady it.

'I'll tell you over dinner. Are you going to open that champagne before it gets warm?'

He twisted the bottle sharply and the cork erupted from the neck of the bottle. The wine spilled over into the glasses and he handed one to her.

She was not making a good job of this. She would have to try much harder. 'Dinner is almost ready,' she said quickly, putting the wine down untasted. 'I'd better check the kitchen.'

'Holly.' His voice stopped her. 'If you've had second thoughts, I'd rather you just said so now. Things got a bit out of hand this morning, but there's no rush.' Seeing the stricken look on her face, he swore softly and then pulled her into his arms. She stiffened instantly, remained rigid as he placed a kiss on her forehead.

He let her go and stepped back, leaving a clear foot between them. But he wasn't angry. In fact his face was so full of sympathy that for a moment she thought he understood, had worked it out for himself. But he didn't, hadn't. Instead he reached into his pocket and took out a small velvet box that lay between them in the palm of his hand.

'What is it?'

He flipped it open to reveal a solitaire diamond that caught the light and sparked with fire. 'It occurred to me that after what happened to Mary I should make my own commitment one hundred per cent clear.' He took the diamond from its velvet nest and took her left hand. 'I thought perhaps we should get this over with first,' he said, 'because I've always thought it to be the height of bad taste to ask a girl to marry you when you're in bed with her. Will you marry me, Holly?'

She thought she might faint. It was so much worse than anything she could have imagined when she was rehearsing what she would say all the long afternoon. The silence stretched out between them, the circle of the ring an inch from the tip of her finger. Then he tossed it up, caught it, dropped it back in his pocket and said a little tersely, 'You don't have to answer straight away. But I thought you should know what my intentions are.'

Now. She must do it now. 'I can't marry you, Joshua.' She saw the brief shaft of pain cross his eyes and moved to touch his arm, without realising what she was doing.

'Brutal, but honest,' he said, withdrawing his arm from her touch.

Honest! Oh, Joshua, her heart wept. I don't want to hurt you; I love you, can't you see that? 'I'm sorry. You are the only man in the world I would ever consider . . . ' This wasn't right. She had to be brutal, although hardly honest. 'But I can't. I don't intend to marry anyone. Just like my mother.' She tried a small laugh, as if this were somehow amusing. It stayed on her lips, quite unable to cover the distance to her eyes.

Joshua did not, apparently, find it funny. His eyes narrowed as he took in the hectic flush of her cheeks, her determined gaiety. 'Will you at least tell me why?' he asked.

'I told you I had some good news.

Wonderful news.' He flinched, but she had to convince him. If he thought she was so stupidly heartless, he would be able to forget her all the more easily. 'Do you remember,' she began, 'that I told you I had visited a sculptor when I was in Florence? That I was thinking of trying something new?'

'I remember.' His voice fell stony hard into her heart, but she had to continue. Had to destroy every vestige of feeling he might have for her.

'Well, I had a phone call from him today. This afternoon. He wants me to go to Italy for a year and study with him. It's the most amazing opportunity. I can hardly believe my luck.'

Dark brows drew together in a frown. 'He phoned you?'

'Yes,' she said, chattering foolishly. 'That's why I'm so glad you're here, because, you see, I've changed my mind about Highfield. I'm going to sell it after all.' Did her voice shake a little? She forced the words out. 'It needs a family, don't you think? Far too big for me. And who knows when I'll come back to England? If ever.' His face was blank. 'But not the land,' she said quickly. 'I want to give the land to the Foundation. Can you handle all that for me?'

'You're really going?' He was finding it hard to believe and she couldn't blame him.

'Oh, yes,' she said, with forced brightness. 'I know you'll understand. I would be an absolute fool to miss this chance. You must seize the moment and I'll never get a chance like this again.' She tried to ignore the puzzled expression in his eyes.

'I'm beginning to understand,' he said, his voice sleety now, and she began to relax. If he despised her, so much the better. 'And when did this — sculptor call?'

'This afternoon,' she said quickly. 'About four o'clock.'

'I see. Then we must celebrate your good fortune.' He handed her the discarded glass of champagne and watched as she gulped at the wine, her throat parched, aching with the strain of lying and tears that she could not shed until he had gone. 'Tell me, Holly,' he said, topping it up. 'This Italian. How did he know where to get in touch with you?'

Lies were hateful things, Holly thought. They always caught you out, especially with someone as clever as Joshua. 'David told him,' she said.

'David?' She expected him to be upset, but now his jaw tightened and the pulse at his temple was hammering angrily. 'I see. You must have given him David's number at his office?'

'Yes,' she said.

'And good old David gave him your number. Well, my dear Holly. To fortune.' He drained his glass and set it down rather hard on the sideboard. He glanced at the table, laid for two with fine china and cutlery, a bowl of flowers filling the room with the heartbreaking scent of early roses. 'You will excuse me if I don't, after all, stay for dinner? I'm going to get drunk now and I prefer to fall into my own bed.' His eyes held hers for a moment. 'Yours, I take it, is no longer on offer?'

He didn't wait for her reply.

11

There was a sickening spin of wheels on the gravel and then the sound of Joshua's Rolls rocketing down the drive. For a moment Holly stood as motionless as the little stone statue of Aphrodite in the garden. Then she just made it to the bathroom before she was violently sick.

After a while she made herself move. She had to clear away the dinner spoiling in the oven. Nothing must remain to provoke any suspicion that she had left the house in distress because Mrs Austin would certainly report anything odd to Joshua, whether he wanted to hear it or not.

Through a film of tears, her hands shaking, she managed to scrape out the pots and put them in the dishwasher. She worked, cleaned the surfaces, scrubbed the sink. It became the most important thing in the world and as long as she concentrated on that she didn't have to think. When the kitchen looked as if it was an illustration from some glossy magazine she at last allowed herself to stop. She was breathing too fast, but she still hadn't finished. There was the dining-room to be tidied. The silver to be put away. It was all so clear in her mind what she had to do. But the crystal flutes that had held the champagne stood together on the table and almost undid her.

She reached out and picked up the rose he had brought her and touched it to her lips. She couldn't understand why Mary had pressed the violets, how she could have borne to see them, to touch them. Something to keep, to remember her lover. She would never forget Joshua, would never forget the warmth of his arms about her, his mouth on hers. It would be a torment for the rest of her life. She dropped the rose in the bin with the champagne bottle and the discarded dinner and let the lid fall back. With that, a kind of grim darkness settled on her.

Only one thing remained to do. She left a note for Mrs Austin, telling her to take the food left in the freezer and the cupboards, and then all the loose ends were tidied away. A few people might raise an eyebrow at her sudden change of plans, but no one would think about it for long.

She took the few belongings she had brought with her, climbed into the sleek black Lotus and drove away into the night.

Just beyond Salisbury she stopped. She couldn't drive any more because for some reason she couldn't see properly. It was a while before she realised it was because she was crying. She sat in the car for a long time, too weak with exhaustion to move, to do anything. Eventually the sun rose and a refreshment stall occupying the same lay-by came to life.

She was still wearing the black chiffon dress, streaked with the marks of her frantic cleaning. It attracted a few stares from lorry drivers stopping for bacon sandwiches and tea, but she didn't care. She sipped a cup of scalding coffee and then got back in her car and drove home. Her real home, where she had always lived. Where she had lived with her own true mother and father who had loved her and cared for her and never done anything to hurt her. And David took one look at her and for once in his life chose discretion.

★　★　★

Life resumed. She couldn't work. Every time she sat before a piece of paper the features of Joshua Kent imposed themselves angrily before her. So instead she expended a surfeit of nervous energy in an orgy of redecoration. Her bedroom first, then David's. She organised the replacement of the guttering and other long outstanding repairs. Even put some insulation into the loft.

Marcus wrote to her. Joshua had gone away, he said, and left him to handle all the details of Highfield. The house, with the garden and studio, had sold immediately and he forwarded the contract for her signature. There was no name shown for the purchaser and, suddenly anxious, she telephoned him from the payphone in the post office.

'Marcus, I have to trust you. But I want Highfield to be used as a proper family home.'

He reassured her. 'I don't have the full details of names, but I didn't want any further delay. Joshua told me that you were going to Italy almost immediately and I wanted it all cleared up before you left.'

The land was being transferred to the Foundation and he asked her if she had time to come to a special ceremony to hand it over, but she declined. 'I'll be away in a few days,' she lied and he didn't make any further effort to persuade her. She signed the contract and sent it back. It was the second hardest thing she had ever done in her life.

A few days later she had an invitation to the summer exhibition at her college. Her head of department had scrawled a note on the back: 'Everyone is dying to show off their triumphs to you, so please come. Love, Harvey.'

She was welcomed enthusiastically by her former students and admired unreservedly everything they had done. One or two of the older women remarked that she had lost some weight and asked if she was looking after herself.

Before she had to think of a suitable answer Harvey spotted her and dragged her off to his office.

'I hoped you'd come tonight. It saves me a journey. I've got a job for you.'

'I don't think I want to come back at the moment,' she said, suddenly panicking at the thought.

He looked at her a little oddly. 'No, it isn't teaching. I'd have you like a shot, you know that, but things are still pretty tight. But I've been asked by a friend if I know anyone who could do a caricature. A really good one. Some High Court judge is retiring and his staff want to give it to him as a present.'

'Rather an odd present,' she said candidly.

He seemed a little disconcerted by this remark. 'I don't know. More original than a clock. Naturally you immediately came to mind and I showed him some of your stuff. Will you do it?' It seemed very important to him, but she shook her head.

'I can't, Harvey. I don't do them any more. You'll have to find someone else.'

'They're a bit short of time.'

She felt as if she was being pushed into doing something she had no appetite for and resisted. 'But I don't know the man. You can't do a good caricature unless you know someone.'

He leapt at this with relief. 'No problem. I explained that, but apparently the old boy is giving a dinner party for his staff at his country home this Saturday and you could go along as a guest of one of the clerks. Stay for the weekend. What do you say?'

'I'd rather not.'

'Well, if you change your mind, let me know before the weekend.'

When she got home David was waiting for her. He had walked around her on tiptoe since her return, taking care over every word, never daring to query her sudden reappearance. But now he clearly had something on his mind and he rushed off to make her a drink, then hovered with the offer of a sandwich. 'No, thanks.' She eyed him cynically. 'Why don't you just tell me what you want? Then we can both relax.'

He grinned awkwardly, relieved that she would at least listen. 'I've a favour to ask you, Holly.'

'Well,' she said, 'there's a surprise.'

He swallowed and pressed on. 'I've met this girl.'

'Yes?' She guessed what was coming, but had no desire to make it easy for him.

'I thought she might spend the weekend here.'

'What you do in your room, David, is your own affair. You know that.'

'I was rather hoping . . . first time and all that.' She was amused to see that he could actually blush. The feeling was so unexpected that she actually smiled.

'You think a landlady on the premises might have a somewhat inhibiting effect? Hasn't she got a place of her own?'

'She shares with a couple of other girls.' He scented victory. 'Come on, Holly, be a sport.'

She sighed. 'When is this scene of depravity to take place?'

'I've asked her over for Saturday.'

'Then your problems are at an end. I have an invitation that, for pity's sake, I apparently have no choice but to accept. But I think it's time you considered moving to a bachelor apartment.'

★ ★ ★

She insisted on taking her own car and followed her 'date' down into the Surrey countryside early on Saturday afternoon. James was a pleasant young man, quite good-looking in a softer, gentler mould than Joshua. He introduced her formally to their host.

'Sir, may I present Miss Holly Carpenter? Holly, The Hon Mr Justice Hedley.'

The judge took her hand and held it for a moment. Despite a lean and vigorous figure, his soft brown hair scarcely dusted with grey, his fingers shook slightly and she wondered if perhaps he was retiring because of bad health.

'Miss Carpenter,' he said at last. 'Welcome to my home. May I call you Holly?'

'Of course, sir.'

'Thank you. Come and have some tea and tell me about yourself.'

She had expected the drawing-room to be full of people arriving for the evening, but they were on their own.

Even her escort had disappeared.

'I understand that you are an artist of some talent, Holly.'

She hadn't expected him to know anything about her; in fact, she was a little surprised that he was paying her any attention at all. 'An artist,' she affirmed. 'The question of talent is for others to pronounce upon. Shall I pour the tea?'

'Yes, thank you. No sugar for me.'

She handed him a cup and poured some for herself and then sat opposite him, taking this opportunity to study the deep character lines of his face. There was a strength forged of some inner pain. A true likeness would not be a comfortable thing to live with, she decided.

'We seem to be a little early, sir. When do the rest of your guests arrive?'

'I'm afraid there are no other guests, my dear. You have been brought here under false pretences and I understand only after a great deal of manoeuvring by your friends.'

The cup paused halfway to her

mouth and she replaced it very carefully on the saucer and set it on the table.

'I think, sir, you had better explain.'

'I wanted to meet you, Holly. I hope you won't be angry with me?'

'I don't understand. Why do you want to meet me? I thought I was here to draw — '

'Yes, I know. But I'm not retiring just yet. There is no dinner party.' He rose swiftly. 'If you've finished with your tea I'd like to show you some of my pictures.'

Puzzled, thoroughly curious and a little bit piqued, she followed him out of the room and across the hall to the library. Over the fireplace hung the portrait of a woman, fair, very English, her sweet face reflected in the flanking portraits of two sons, one of whom was the young man who had brought her to the house.

'James is your son?'

'Yes. He's my son. I've been very lucky with both the boys. His brother is a doctor.'

'I'm sorry. I understood — was told,' she corrected herself, 'that he was your clerk.'

'A slight deception on my part. I hope you'll forgive me, Holly?'

'Forgive you?' Holly was suddenly, painfully angry at being deceived by people she considered to be friends and the emotion jolted through her like lightning. It was the first time she had felt anything in weeks. But she had been somehow tricked into coming to this man's house and she wanted to know why. She turned from the portrait in front of her and said stiffly, 'If I haven't come here to draw a picture of you, sir, then perhaps you would be good enough to tell me exactly what is the purpose of my visit.'

He smiled then, for the first time. 'You are so like your mother. Not just in looks, although it is just as well I was warned how alike you were or I would have completely disgraced myself when you walked through the door. Then Jamie might well have suspected that you were a little more than the daughter of an old friend. But in your manner, too. Absolutely straightforward. She was like that.'

Holly's skin prickled uneasily. 'You knew my mother?' she asked. And she knew it was Mary he was talking about.

'Yes, Holly. I knew your mother.' His expression was watchful, grave. 'In every sense of the word.'

He took a notebook from his pocket and handed it to her. A book covered with Chinese brocade. Holly swallowed a cry. 'Where did you get this?' It should be at home. Back in the loft. She had braved the spiders and replaced the evidence of her birth in its hiding place. Her mouth tightened. David, still trying to flush out a story. All that nonsense about a new girlfriend. And somehow he had managed to involve Harvey. 'Who are you?' she demanded.

'My name is Andrew Hedley. In her journal, Mary referred to me as 'A' in an attempt to hide my true identity. Clearly she was unsuccessful. Mr Kent had very little trouble in finding me.' He walked across to a padded window-seat and held out a hand, inviting her to join him. She moved on stiff, unwilling legs, the reality of what he said slow to sink in. 'It's odd, you know. I always wanted a daughter. My wife gave me a brace of sons but then there were complications and she couldn't manage any more. She gave me all this, too. I'm afraid I had the best of the deal.' He looked out over the extensive parkland. 'She's a wonderful woman and I do love her.'

'Do you?' Holly asked stiffly.

'Yes, my dear. It's quite possible, you know, to love two women. It was never a wild passion. There's only room for one, I think, in a lifetime and Mary took up all of that.' He paused, going away a little in his head at the contemplation of the awesome difference. 'But I do love her and she's never given me any reason to doubt that she loves me. She came to me as the perfect wife for a struggling barrister. Good connections, plenty of money. It was a family arrangement and I tried to be a good husband. After Mary . . . ' He paused as if even the words hurt, then gathered himself again. 'After Mary sent me packing, it was easy.'

'Mary sent you . . . she was the one to break off the affair?'

'I'm afraid so. I went to Ashbrooke determined to take her away with me. Start again somewhere new.'

Holly stared around her at the beautiful Tudor manor, the vast acres stretching away into the distance. 'You would have given up all this for her?'

'Without a second thought,' he said, so fervently that she knew without doubt he was speaking the truth.

Her heart was beating very fast. Too fast. 'Why wouldn't she go with you?'

'Because she knew it would destroy my career. I was already a recorder. I was pointed at the top.' He smiled at an old memory. 'She was very clever about it. She knew that if she said it was for my own good I wouldn't listen. So she told me that she had met someone else. She was going to get married.'

'And you actually believed her?' She glanced at the book with its burning outflow of passion and found it hard to accept.

His eyes, amber like her own, followed her gaze. 'She was very convincing. She hurt me so badly. Twisted the knife. Laughed at me. I left without looking back, hating her.' Holly almost cried out. She bit her lip in a desperate need to keep the sound in and Andrew Hedley looked at her with deep concern. 'I'm sorry; this has been a shock. I think perhaps I'd better get you a drink.'

'No!' she stopped him. 'Just tell me.'

He looked doubtful, but then, after a moment in which her eyes begged him, he continued. 'It was years before I found out that she had been lying. I saw her photograph in one of the papers. When she launched her charity.'

Holly looked down at her hands, the notebook twisting between her fingers.

'Did you see her then?'

'No. What could I say? It was over. Years over. And I still have a wife. Hurting one woman in a lifetime is enough guilt for one man to live with.'

'I thought you had abandoned her.'

'And hated me for it?' She didn't answer, but he didn't need an answer. 'Respect her decision, Holly. She knew that if we took my way it would destroy us both. She set me free. And now I have the chance to get to know a daughter that I never knew I had. If she will allow it?'

'But what about your family? Do they know? Have you told them?'

He shook his head. 'Not yet. Who you are, Holly, is your story. I gave up every right to ask you to acknowledge me as your father the day I let a young woman bamboozle me with a pack of loving lies. But I'll tell them now.'

'No, sir. I'd rather you didn't.' Pain crossed his strong features and she reached out and touched his hand. 'That's not a rejection of you. But you have a family. Mary made her decision and lived with it. We must both live with it. I'm sure she never regretted it. And I had good parents who loved me.' She smiled tentatively. 'Stick to your story. I am, after all, the daughter of an old friend.' Like her mother, she had made a decision to drive away the man she loved. Unlike Mary, she had been wrong. But she, too, would have to live with it. There was at least a little consolation to be gained from knowing the truth.

The library door opened and Jamie put his head around it. 'Sir, mother's asking for you. She wants to know how many people will be staying for dinner.'

'Thank you, Jamie, I'll come now. Look after Holly, will you? Show her to her room. The blue bedroom.'

Jamie looked startled. 'But . . . '

'The blue bedroom, Jamie.'

'Yes, sir.' Jamie led Holly up the wide staircase, chatting amiably about nothing much. She watched him. Saw his father in him now. He was still young.

Another ten years and his features, too, would harden with the demands of his career.

He stopped by a door deeply inset in the panelling. 'This is the blue room. If you need anything, just pick up the house phone.' He smiled awkwardly, as if he had been caught out in some prank he wasn't very proud of. 'I'll see you at dinner.'

'Thank you, Jamie.'

She watched him turn and walk quickly away. Jamie might not know the truth about her, but he knew more than Andrew Hedley had told her. She glanced down at the book in her hand, wondering how her father had come by it. Somehow, she didn't think David would have parted with it. They would talk again tomorrow. Surely then everything would be clear.

She caught the handle impatiently and opened the door, halfway through before she stopped abruptly, realising there was someone already in the room. A broad back, a dark head staring out of the window at the park.

'Come in, Holly. And shut the door.'

The room began to close in and the blood pounding through her head was louder and louder until she thought her ears would burst with the pressure. Then, thankfully, everything went black.

The cold flannel on her forehead dragged her back into semi-consciousness and she tried to open her eyes.

'Joshua? What are you doing here?'

'Hush. You'll be fine in a minute. Just lie still.' Her head ached dreadfully and she had no confidence in that remark. But she did as she was told because moving would be too much effort.

The bed moved slightly under his weight as he sat beside her and she protested weakly as he undid the top button of her blouse and loosened her waistband. But he ignored her complaint and it felt so much better that she didn't care.

'Did I faint?'

'Yes, my love. I'm afraid you did. When you're better you can ring a peal about my ears for giving you such a fright.'

'I wasn't frightened. It was the shock . . . ' Too many shocks for one day. 'How did you find out?'

'How did I find out why you ran away from me?' he asked.

'That will do for a start.'

'It took a while, Holly. Your sudden and complete turn-about rather numbed my thinking cells. I thought, hoped, that you loved me and to be quite that wrong about anyone is totally unnerving. And then you lied to me about the phone call and for a while I was so angry that I didn't actually care why.'

She stared at him. 'How did you know I lied?'

'Because, my sweet, idiotic, beautiful Holly, David could not possibly have given anyone your telephone number that Saturday.'

'Oh?' she said, cross that her subterfuge had been so easily seen through.

'Oh?' he mocked her gently. 'I'll tell

you why. Because David Grantham never went back to his office on Saturday. He made it as far as Ashbrooke Hall and decided he was a danger to himself and other road users and very wisely took a room for the rest of the day in order to catch up on some sleep. He was just leaving when I got back from Exeter, over the moon with happiness and that damned ring almost burning a hole in my pocket.'

'Oh, David!'

'Not a man to be relied upon, Holly,' he warned her. 'And very easily browbeaten into becoming an ally. How else do you think I would have got into your house and helped myself to Mary's book?'

'How did you know where to look for it?'

'Inspired guesswork. And you apparently left the ladder on the upstairs landing for David to put away. Careless.'

'I'm sorry, Joshua. I had to do it. I couldn't think of any other way.' She was beginning to feel a little less faint and moved up against the pillows.

'I can see how everything must have slotted into place when you saw that photograph. Mrs Austin told me that you asked three times if my father's name was Alexander. Quite odd, she said. I had to see the notebook, of course, but it didn't take much working out.'

'No. But how did you know it wasn't the truth?'

He took her chin and lifted it gently so that she was forced to face him. 'I telephoned my father, Holly, and asked him.'

She went pale. 'Mrs Austin said your mother had a lot to put up with . . . ' she mumbled. 'I shouldn't have listened.'

'My father had a long rein, Holly. But he always knew who was holding it. And he confined his affairs to ladies who knew the score. He wasn't in the market for the kind of complication that an affair with Mary would have involved. And my mother loved him despite all his faults.'

'But you said . . . '

He let his hand fall. 'I know what I said. That my father carried a torch for Mary. And it was true. After my mother died, Mary was very good to him. I thought for a while that they might have made something of it. But she was clearly a one-man woman.'

'I'm sorry,' she whispered.

'Don't be. Anyone might have leapt to the same conclusion.' He brushed the hair back from her face. 'Feeling better?' She nodded and after a moment he went on. 'But the thing is, Holly, after he got over the shock, my father was able to suggest who the mysterious 'A' might be. Andrew Hedley stayed with us whenever he came for the quarter sessions. My father saw Mary and him together once, up on the moor. They were just walking together, but clearly it was surprising enough to stick in his mind.' He smiled slightly. 'I thought, in the circumstances, that it might be best not to question his own presence there.'

'So you knew him?'

'Only as someone I had to be very polite to. I had no idea his name was Andrew. But when I confronted him with the notebook he admitted it immediately. If only you'd let me look for him when I first offered . . . ' She groaned and he caught her up in his arms and held her close. 'Unless, of course, you prefer me as a brother?' His eyes glittered inches from her own.

It would be so easy to be swept away on that tide of passion he woke in her with such frightening ease. But she held herself rigid. 'That rather depends.'

'I see.' He stepped back, and his look became detached, as if he was preparing himself for something so awful he would need every ounce of strength to keep his feelings hidden. 'If you still have doubts, Holly, I'd like to hear them. I think this time you should give me the opportunity to defend myself.'

'Yes. No more hidden doubts.' Holly

317

had no doubts about her own love. She was ready to open her arms and her heart, but he had been so unconcerned by his father's unfaithfulness and she remembered all too clearly the look in Lisa Stamford's eye when they had met in the reception hall at Ashbrooke Hall that first evening. She was exactly the sort of woman who 'knew the score'. 'I love you, Joshua,' she said evenly. 'With all my heart. Wait!' She held him back when he would have drawn her into his arms again. 'I have to tell you that I'm not like your mother. I could never look the other way, Joshua. If you want a long rein, then we have no future together.'

He gripped her arms quite painfully. 'Marry me, Holly, and you'll need no rein to keep me by your side. I love you. There will never be anyone else. You've turned my life upside-down and that's the way I like it.'

It was the truth. Absolute and direct. She raised her arms to him. 'Then why are we still talking?'

'Because, my darling, we need to get a few things straight while I'm still capable of stringing a coherent sentence together.' He produced the velvet box from his pocket. 'Shall we try again?'

'Yes, please.' He took the ring from the box and once again held it at the tip of her finger, then raised his eyes to hers.

'Will you marry me, Holly?' She nodded, quite unable to speak with happiness. He slipped it on and turned her hand slightly so that the sunlight flashed and broke in a thousand sparks. And then he kissed her.

It was Holly who finally realised there was someone knocking at the door and pushed Joshua away. 'Come in,' she called as he quickly stood up.

Andrew Hedley glanced from his daughter, taking in the dishevelled state of her clothes, to the man standing beside the bed. There was a certain chill in his voice as he said, 'I take it that all confusion is at an end, Mr Kent?'

'Yes, sir,' Joshua said. 'But this isn't

what you're thinking. Holly fainted . . . '

'And you were giving her the kiss of life?'

Holly laughed and struggled up from the bed. 'Something like that.' She went across to the older man and took his hands. 'Will you do something for me?' she asked. 'A very special favour.'

He nodded, his face softening. 'Anything.'

'When I marry Joshua, will you give me away?'

'My dear, dear Holly. It will be my honour.'

★ ★ ★

Joshua's father decided to stay on in England for a few weeks after the wedding and lent them his house for their honeymoon. But now it was over and as the car approached Ashbrooke Joshua was very quiet.

Holly glanced at him once or twice, then put her hand on his arm. 'What is it, darling?'

320

'I've been thinking about the stable flat. You do realise that it isn't going to be big enough for the two of us?'

'It will be for a while. After all, we'll be in London for a lot of the time.'

He wasn't convinced. 'Will you ever forgive me for selling the Hall? It should have been yours.'

She laughed. 'Don't be silly. I couldn't possibly live in a place like that.'

'You're sure?' he asked.

'Positive. I'd hate it. And that four-poster bed.'

His eyes glinted. 'I think you could get to like it. Now you've given up wearing nightgowns.'

She blushed. 'We'll never know.'

'Pity.'

'Yes.' She glanced quickly away to hide a tear of regret for Highfield.

'Unless this would do?' He offered her a long manila envelope.

She glanced at it and frowned. 'What is it?'

'A slightly belated wedding-present. I

should have given it to you before, but somehow we always had something more interesting to do.'

The document slipped on to her lap and even before she read the words she knew what it was. She turned to him. 'You bought Highfield! But how . . . ? Oh, it doesn't matter.' She flung her arms about his neck. 'Oh, Joshua, how can I ever thank you?'

'I can think of any number of ways, my love,' he murmured into her neck. He glanced at the chauffeur, who kept his eyes fixed very firmly upon the road. 'But I think we'd better wait until we get home before I let you try.' His kiss was sweet and lingering. A promise. 'But I'd better warn you, there have been one or two alterations since your last visit.'

'Oh,' she said dangerously.

'To the main bedroom. It had to be redecorated.'

'It was perfect!'

'For a single lady, perhaps. I've changed the furniture. When I sold the

Hall to Luigi I decided I simply couldn't bear to part with — '

'That rotten bed!'

'How can you be so unfeeling? I fell in love with you in that bed. I don't know how I stopped myself from climbing in with you then and there.'

'Really?' she asked, touched by this declaration.

'Positively. In fact I intend to show you. Just as soon as we get home.'

THE END

Working at Moonbeam Lake, it wasn't easy for single mother Laura Matthews. She wanted her twins to enjoy summer in the place she'd once loved — despite its painful memories. But she hadn't counted on Tanner Mcleod's reappearance. Six years ago, she'd comforted him when his brother died, and it had led to passion. But Tanner had left before she'd discovered the consequences of their love. How could she confess that *he* was the father the twins had never met?

KNAVE OF DIAMONDS

Wendy Kremer

Sharon is employed by a retailer to write some PR text about Patrick, a famous jewellery designer, who's creating an exclusive collection for the everyday woman. Patrick's initial resentment of Sharon changes when he gets to know her, whilst she admits that he's a fascinating man. If only other women didn't think so too! Then as Sharon and Patrick visit Hong Kong for a photo session things begin to buzz — only to fall apart. What has fate designed for them?

TAKE A CHANCE ON LOVE

Claire Dalton

After returning to her home town, Catherine Earnshaw plans to spend all her time on her job at the local newspaper and caring for her elderly father. One thing she's sure of is that there's no room for a man in her new life. She's been hurt once before and she daren't allow herself to fall for the enigmatic Sean Bradford-Jones, or rely on him when all her plans start to unravel . . .

THE TREASURE SEEKERS

Anne Holman

Not comfortable with the genteel life of a spinster in Bath, Frances longs to go and find her father, Professor Arthur Cannon, presumed missing whilst on a plant-hunting mission in Central America. To her mother's dismay Frances happily joins her aunt and uncle on an expedition to the Gulf of Mexico. On the way she meets the intriguing, but secretive, George Webster. Her adventures begin, but will she find her father — and can she also find love?

A MATTER OF PRIDE

Margaret Mounsdon

Working for the opera star Bede Evans and his glamorous wife Jasmine is the perfect job for Rhianna O'Neill — until she inherits a wilful sixteen-year-old half sister after the tragic death of their mother in an accident . . . Then Rhianna's life is shattered by her broken engagement to Sax, Bede and Jasmine's son, and she takes off for France with handsome Luc Fermier, an old flame from her past. But that is when her problems really begin . . .

PLACE OF HEALING

Paula Williams

When talented cook Jess is betrayed by her boyfriend and best friend, she has to get away, so she books a holiday cottage in a remote corner of Somerset. And Higher Neston immediately feels like home, her landlady Elsie like family. Jess lacks confidence in her own instincts, yet finding herself caught in the middle of family quarrels and old rivalries, she must learn to listen to her heart and decide who is trustworthy . . .